5-2(

PACIFIC TREMORS

PACIFIC TREMORS

RICHARD STERN

TRIQUARTERLY BOOKS
NORTHWESTERN UNIVERSITY PRESS | EVANSTON, ILLINOIS

TriQuarterly Books
Northwestern University Press
Evanston, Illinois 60208-4210

Printed in the United States of America

10 9 8 7 6 5 4 3 2 1

ISBN 0-8101-5131-6

Library of Congress Cataloging-in-Publication Data

Stern, Richard G., 1928–
Pacific tremors / Richard Stern.
p. cm.
ISBN 0-8101-5131-6
1. Hollywood (Los Angeles, Calif.)—Fiction. 2. Motion
picture industry—Fiction. 3. Friendship—Fiction.
4. Death—Fiction. I. Title.
PS3569.T39 P28 2001
813'.54—dc21
2001005116

Much of this book was written at the Center for Advanced Study in the Behavioral Sciences (Stanford, California) from September 1999 to June 2000 and is gratefully, affectionately, and nostalgically dedicated to the genial Fellows of that year and the wonderful officers and staff who help every Fellow every year.

I also wish to acknowledge my dear friend from Chapel Hill days, Edgar Bowers, who introduced me to California in 1964 and who died in San Francisco on February 4, 2000, in his seventy-sixth year.

Like most of my work these last thirty years, this book owes more than I know how to acknowledge to my beloved wife, Alane Rollings.

CONTENTS

PACIFIC TREMORS

★   ★   ★   ★

It is almost a decade since I found myself for the price of a ten-cent admission fee in a little motion picture theater on Broadway. As I assumed a seat, a player piano was attacking a Johann Strauss waltz, "Voices from the Vienna Woods." Upon the floor, a squalid puddle of peanut shells.

Around me, men, women, and children divided the sustained comfort of chewing gum with the fleeting rapture of the nut.

One decade ago. And the film! A two-reel Drama of the West. As I regarded its palsied agitation, there rose in my mind images of the beauteous Carmen entrancing that poor twig of infantry, Don José; the Gascon D'Artagnan taking honorable place with the dashing trio, Aramis, Porthos, and Athos; the bold Henry Esmond crossing the channel with the Young Pretender.

Why should not every Great Novel, Drama, and Opera of the world be transmitted in the One Language that needs no translation?

. . . When I left the theater that bright November day, I was no longer the humble neckware salesman from Schenectady, I was—thanks to the power of the motion picture and that imperfect implement, the Human Brain—halfway to what I would soon be, H. Dannmeyer Fishman of Megalo-Fishman-Wolff.

From *Ad Astra Per Aspera:*
The Autobiography of H. D. Fishman, 1922
(Macmillan, 1923)

LEET AND KENERET ★ In the Pacific

Leet's latest offer had come from an elderly American who'd watched her playing tennis with Gretchen, the manager of the resort. When they changed sides the first time, he'd asked, "Do you mind if I watch? I love good tennis."

"If you think ve're good, then certainly vatch us," said Gretchen, who, like Leet, had come to Fiji from Europe. To Leet, she said, "You don't mind an admirer of your serf and folly, do you?"

"Suit yourself, sir," said Leet.

When they made good shots, the man applauded, and when they shook hands at the end of the match, he asked if he could buy them a drink.

"Not me, sank you fery much," said Gretchen. "I must pick up guests at Suva. But perhaps Mademoiselle de Loor could use an Orange Crush."

Accustomed to lust for her person, Leet had learned to deflect it without serious disturbance to the lusters. Keneret's offer, though made quickly and casually, was made with a weight of seriousness unusual enough not to be given the automatic, if courteous, turndown. "Would you be fooling a girl, Mr. Keneret?"

Leet had seen all sorts of people from all sorts of places in this, for many of them, remotest of places, but mostly she saw fair, open-faced Aussies and Kiwis. In Keneret, there was something ingrown and cautiously self-regarding; something in the black eyes and lined forehead that made him seem another order of being. It was hard to tell how old he was, maybe sixty, yet there was something unfinished and unsure in him, and something else too, something powerful. It was in his speech which was full of qualification and in his hoarse yet mellifluous voice. "I would, I have, but not now, not you. You're not the usual girl, not in looks and— my guess—other ways."

"I failed the *bac*. Is that unusual enough?"

"That, no. Your telling me, yes. In any event, I guarantee nothing, but if you have half as much talent—we can talk about what that means—as you clearly have brains, beauty, and grace, you'd have a shot at, well, something you might like."

They sat across the counter from each other, Leet backed by the little world of her business: the yellow and black cylinders of tennis balls, the soft-drink fridge, the pegged board on which the strung and unstrung rackets hung, the clipboard with the diagrammed pages of Round Robins and tennis lessons. Behind Keneret were the orange-red courts, the coconut palms, hibiscus, oleander, bougainvillea, and guava trees, the heavy blue sky, the conical green hills, the wooden bungalows and tended lawns of Pacific Resorts' Naviti Hotel. Leet's address these last four years.

It was time, she'd been thinking, to get another. Life was bearable, even pleasant, but the days were like waves: they rolled on, broke, and vanished. There was no progress, no shape to them or to her life. It was flat as her body, serviceable and mobile, but that wasn't enough. Even if it were perfect—it wasn't—what did it have to do with what counted?

At the hotel this week was a young—younger than she—Aussie football player, here with his team for a match in Suva. His ribs were bandaged, most of the rest of him bare. He proposed a swim at high tide; she'd said okay. A sex hour with a transient was her speed, enough to give point to a day, maybe two days. But a week? A season? A life?

"What would it be like?" she asked Keneret. "I don't know anything about movies. I don't even see them here. What does one do? And first, do I have to—is it that you want me to go to bed with you?"

"I do," said Keneret. "But I don't make it a part of the other. I'd have too much trouble that way. I'll tell you what you have to know. At the worst, you'll learn something about the business."

In her white shorts and slate-blue tennis shirt, the girl with the odd name was a stunning anomaly here in the middle of the Pacific. It was as if one of the jungle-covered hills had turned into a sixty-story Hilton. (The way things went, that was more likely.) Her short toast-colored hair, green eyes, flip nose, lips, ears, chin, slim legs, slight breasts, and beautiful movement on the court seemed to this professional user of scenic talent wasted here. Suppose she were a Chris Evert, marooned forever in the Pacific? (She wasn't. Though her formal strokes were perfect, she missed lots of shots—and showed a grand amateur temper when she did.)

Mademoiselle de Loor. Leet.

"Short for Aletheia, 'One Who Tells the Truth.' My father knew old Greek."

"Was he a professor?"

"A journalist. Look here, sir, I've got to give lessons now, but, if you wish, we may have a drink in the Wauwausawu Room. Six o'clock."

[2]

The theory underlying the erotic power of movies was that if a person appealed to an experienced moviemaker, she or he might appeal to the audience of his films. There were a few hundred hours in twenty-odd cities that were special to Keneret because of it. Especially in his first movie years, talent searches often ended in the sack. Unlike, say, Floyd Harmel, he was no world-class screwer, but again unlike Floyd, he didn't delude himself about the sexual power of his job. Even now, at seventy, Floyd claimed that many of the women who ended up in his bed didn't know who he was or what he did: "She thought I was just some old wacko, but"—spreading thick forearms—"she liked me."

In the Wauwausawu Room, Keneret imagined telling his old Englishman friend, the movie critic Wendell Spear, about meeting Leet. *We're in this thatch-roofed, open-to-the-winds room, a bar in the back, waitresses in grass bras and skirts. In front, a causeway to a three-tree is-land. Black-and-green birds flying in and out of cliffs; coral reefs poking out of a very blue ocean. Pure* dolce far niente, *especially with a booze buzz and a Javanese cigar.* (He'd bought a box for Wendell.) *I almost for-got where I was, what I was. An advantage of decrepitude: the need's too weak to make you miserable.*

So, Spear might say, *you rolled out your Hollywood carpet. What then?*
To that, he didn't yet have an answer.

[3]

Leet apologized for not changing. "They save a room for me in the lodge—when they have it, but they're booked up. I've got my own bun-galow in Segatoku." *A lovely voice*—to the imagined Spear—*with that odd rising pitch and those off-center vowels that tell you she grew up speaking French.* "So I couldn't take a shower." Making a French girl's adorable moue. "Forgive me."

He imagined her in the shower. *One of those times,* he'd tell Spear, *when you'd give up a toe to be thirty-five or forty. She ordered and drank what she said she'd invented, rum and kava. Kava's the local brew. Awful, water after you've done the wash in it.*

You were stirred by her.

She interested me. Looks, speech, her being there. Her story. You know there's always a story.

Three nights ago, his first here, Keneret was asked by a young waitress where he came from. "Los Angeles," he'd said.

"So you're a Spain man."

Surprised, then amused, Keneret thought, "Why should she know any more of the U.S. than I of her country? After all, it has a history." Before he'd left the States, he'd spent ten minutes skimming the Fiji entry in *Bri-tannica.* (He'd spent half an hour on "Australia.") All he remembered was a series of wars with Tonga, which lacked the wood that these islands had. There had also been the British bringing Indian coolies to build the roads; their descendants owned most of the shops and divided govern-ment rule with the Poly- and Melanesians who'd made those star-guided longboat voyages over the Pacific. There'd been coups, a colonial period, and, since the end of World War II, independence. In short, a full history of the sort one studied in school; but for Keneret, the point of the island was that it was out of history, a spot of vacation—*emptiness*—en route from Sydney (where he'd failed to get financing for a film on Burley Griffin, the designer of Canberra, and then stood in for Floyd at the latest Harmel Festival).

Leet's story was a part of history which, for Keneret, had blood in it.

"For years," said Leet, "We didn't know we were abandoned. That word wasn't in our vocabulary." "We" meant Mama and brother Marc. They lived "in the country" while Papa worked as a journalist in Paris, where, as a very young man, he had been important. How important was the question with which a tribunal confronted him and for which, finally, he was fined and censured but not imprisoned. A brilliant twenty-two-year-old ministerial assistant out of the École Normale, he'd helped write the first statute of racial specificity in modern French history, the one which defined Jews as criminal outcasts. *This little beauty's father! The Technicolor of the place flushed into black and white like those newsreel flashbacks of Marcel Ophuls.*

"I was nine when Papa's letter came from Argentina. It said he had had no choice, we would be—do you say 'hunted'? 'hounded'?—as he was being, unless he left. And there was the sentence—it was so terrible for us—to 'look upon your husband and your father as a page torn out of your lives.' *Figurez vous.*" *She stopped a bit; I thought she wouldn't go on, but I said nothing, just waited, sympathetic.*

Keneret imagined that Pieter de Loor would have liked the page torn out of his own life, but since 1966, when, said Leet, the book that devoted a chapter to his work on the racial statute was published, he must have thought that it would be the only page for which he'd be remembered. So the three De Loors knew that they'd been abandoned by a suddenly notorious father whom they loved and who—they were sure—loved them.

Keneret, who'd thought much about the many feelings called love, thought that in a film the Leet character would have a lot to learn. The learning would be the story line.

"In the country, we lived in the house where Mama and Grandmama had been born," one of forty inhabited houses of Meillac-en-Gers, the heart of old Gascony, to which her mother's grandfather had come as schoolmaster in the 1890s. Meillac was what Leet knew, stone houses with walls so thick the hottest days didn't pierce them, and in winter so cold that only heavy socks and sweaters could keep the blood running. Meillac was sheep, cows, horses, ducks, geese—force-fed for foie gras—dogs, flies, swallows, crows, hills, fields of maize, fences, the graveyard, the church, the war monument, and the one-room school—fifteen students—founded by Mama's grandfather. In Leet's last years there, there was a public telephone cabinet, which, with television and newspapers from Miélan, the nearby town, linked their village remoteness to the great world.

Leet was not a skilled storyteller. It was as if every word that came out of her was a surprise to the ones that came before. Perhaps, thought Keneret, it's her telling it in English. *She was seeing it in a new way,* said the imaginary Spear. Keneret said, "But all that happened long before you were born."

"What?" Shaking herself to see not just a screen of sympathy on which she'd projected her story but a dark, elderly, inquisitive, male face. "I don't understand—"

"The trial, the tribunal, when they didn't send him to prison. Wasn't that fifteen years or more before you were born?"

"Yes. And no one spoke about it, though I knew it was why Papa didn't work here—*there*—in Meillac and only visited us. Even if there'd been work for a journalist. The old people knew. He'd never been their favorite, always *le flamand,* though his father had come to Bordeaux before World War One, fought in the French army, and spoke pure French. After the book, after *Figaro* and *La Gazette de Tarbes* took it up, something changed. Even my friends looked at me bizarrely. Papa was younger than I am now when he wrote that law. If he wrote it. I have no idea; I didn't read the book. Nothing he said to me was ever like that. Maybe that's what made him think he'd never be free of it. He thought he'd given up enough, making this life for himself in Paris and only visiting us. Sometimes he talked about going off somewhere with us when he'd saved enough. He came maybe once a month. Every visit was like a holiday. It made it very hard to lose when we knew we'd lost it; lost him. Mama only said that Papa had been deep in things he'd been too young to understand. But she smelled of abandonment. I think people smell of what happens to them. So we maybe smelled too."

"I'm a poor smeller," said Keneret. "I wouldn't know."

"It's part of you, like cold and white are parts of snow. *Abandoned.* That's what you are. I don't know what the abandoner smells like. Maybe nothing. Papa believed that he did the right thing: going away so we wouldn't be part of it. If he'd come back to the village, the hatred would spread to us. Abandoned, we'd be pitied. It's safe to be pitied. He thought that that was the last thing he could give us. I don't judge what he did, didn't try, don't try. Marc read the book and said Papa was *un collabo.* The word meant nothing to me. Maybe I'm a coward, an ostrich hiding her head? Was Papa?"

Keneret, feeling in her face something beyond him, said, "The ostrich knows it's his most valuable part, so he protects it. *Heroism* and *cowardice* may not be the right words." This sagacity did not seem to register. "What about your mama?"

Leet looked into her drink, and Keneret at the beautiful ellipse of her bent neck. To see her like a painting in this place with the green and black birds flying in and out of the cliffs above the blue ocean was enchanting. What a shot it would be. "I guess she ostriched, too, but not by hiding. She became the village—do you say 'nosebody'? Busy with everybody's life. And her own. She milked the goats and cows, sewed, crocheted, painted furniture, watered and weeded the vegetables, gossiped, read the newspaper, listened to the radio, bought the first television set in the village. Everybody came in to watch. She tried making Armagnac; one of the few things that failed. Busy, busy. Some keep busy, some silent; some run. I'm like Papa. As soon as I could, I ran. I first thought that I'd run after him, to Argentina, then I thought, 'You'll make trouble, he could have a new life and wife.' I know nothing about that even now. I hardly know what I feel. Except sometimes. Sometimes I hate him. Sometimes I want to see him so much it's like that feeling in your bones when you have fever."

Keneret forced himself to keep from touching her face. "He was obviously a brilliant young man. Maybe he's made another brilliant career. Do you know if he's alive?"

"Do you think I'd hear if something happened to him?"

"Probably yes, though I'd guess that he lives quietly down there."

"Whatever, it's his life. I have mine. I went to *collège*, though I didn't succeed in the *bac*, and after I discovered tennis, didn't try a second time. I watched the matches from Roland Garros; then I bought a racket. Usually I'm awkward, but not so much on court. Forehands, backhands, overheads, that's what it seems I can do. I won a tournament in Tarbes. I coached in a Club. When Mama died, Marc and I sold the house. The English were buying houses all over the countryside. We sold it for two hundred thousand francs. Two weeks later, I saw the advertisement of Pacific Resorts in *Figaro* which got me here. And here I stay, playing tennis, speaking English." She looked into his face, blushed, looked away, and said, "Maybe I'll add: Then I met an American film director who said, 'You can be in the movies.'"

Director.

The word restored Keneret to his position. He'd been lost in the girl's story, one of thousands that came out of those eruptions of the thirties and forties. Almost half a century later, the world hadn't put them to bed. They were built into the postwar world like the stones of Augustan Rome into modern Rome's walls. This boyish beauty with the flip nose and short hair had brought her father's story out here to be washed by a million square miles of the Pacific. Swinging her racket, tootling around in her VW under the jungle-covered cones of the coral island, she was as far away from those old hatreds as she could be on earth, which wasn't, it seemed, far enough.

[4]

Keneret had spent most of his adult life on the semitropical shores of the Pacific, but his Asian linkage was weak. He'd spent weeks touring, scouting, even working up a few deals in half a dozen Asian countries, but he knew no Pacific or Oriental language and next to none of the countries' histories or literature. He knew some Chinese and Japanese films, had met Ozu, Kurosawa, Mifune, and that beautiful Gong girl, had read a few novels—Tanizaki, Mishima, Kawabata—and a few old Chinese poems which his wife, Marcia, a poetry reader, elucidated for him, but here too he was a tourist, enjoying impressions whose exoticism amused or re-pelled him without making the kind of sense almost every American im-pression did. If Oriental ways were the future, he was far more lost than he often felt now in the Hollywood run by thirty-year-old M.B.A.'s and graduates of film schools who grew up making movies with Panoflex and editing on digital tape. Wendell Spear had written a piece on this trans-formed Hollywood, calling it "The Pacification of Films," by which—he told Keneret—he meant the "invisible dominance of a Pacific mentality, indolent nihilism masked by passionately phony ideology and ferocious deal making." Spear, purer than anyone who actually made movies could afford to be, believed that the Pacification began when Technicolor took over and would end—he, somewhat fancifully, wrote—"*With interactive, Huxleyan feelies, the sense-mad audience assimilated into the copulations and knifings of a so-called 'virtual reality.' In short,*" ended his jeremiad, "*the actual, not virtual, death of the imagination.*"

"Your story," Keneret told Leet, "might make a film, or part of one. Would you be willing to write it up? An outline, if you like."

"I write two letters a year. In French. And it takes me a month to get ready to write one. Anyway, I don't know what the story is. How does it even end?"

"Don't worry about the end. We supply those."

"I didn't know you were thinking of me as a writer."

"I wasn't. You're a striking young woman."

"Striking?"

"Strong. Vivid. Lovely."

"Thank you."

"You might film wonderfully. Did you ever model?"

"No."

"Doesn't matter. You have a cameo clarity." His hand carved a profile in the air. "Very fine chisel work there. I think you'd photograph well." He brought the hand across the table to her cheek, touched it, and with-drew. Though her face didn't move, it had withdrawn. "You seem—iso-lated out here. Or—your word—'abandoned.' To me. Though what do I know? I know L.A., I know Honolulu, a bit of Tokyo and Sydney, but Naviti Bay? This is off the flight plan. A flight of fancy. Know that term?"

She shook her head for no. "Something in the air," he waved his hands in the air, spiraling. "It's hard to imagine it as anything but a set for a musical comedy. Rodgers and Hammerstein did one."

[5]

What was this old American talking about? He'd waved a gold passport at her. Was he taking it away? That's what she got for opening up to him. Her story disgusted him. She should have told him Gretchen's story. It wasn't all that different, except that Gretchen's father was Austrian and a soldier and hadn't disappeared but stayed home and died the way fathers are supposed to. There were millions with the same story, children and grandchildren of dirty history. "I've never acted, not even in a school play. I don't think I'd be good at pretending."

"Some of the best movie actors aren't either. Movie acting is just a way of being yourself. Some good stage actors fall on their faces. Then somebody walks in from the street, and the camera loves her. I've had lots of experience, but I can't tell when it'll happen. The eye isn't a camera. I should've had footage—film—of you while you were telling your story."

"I wouldn't have told it."

"I'll take some of you walking, talking. We'll see what happens. Don't hope. One in a thousand works out."

But she'd already hoped, and something switched off in her face. "Don't bother. You'll just waste your film."

Switches were going on and off in him as well. He was angry at himself. He'd made this lovely young person unhappy. Who did he think he was, Zeus, spotting a milkmaid in the hills and swanning down to shoot his almighty godhood into her?

★　　★　　★　　★

"Garbo," said Maman, "was a thick-legged Svenska sales-girl on whom the film gods dripped angel dust. Stiller and Pabst discovered that the thickness melted away in close-ups. Clumsy, she couldn't move without tripping over her huge feet, so they kept her still. With that and a few filters, they invented Garbo. Mayer spotted her and brought her to Metro. A tough guy, but she squeezed him like an orange, got him to pay her a fortune. Of course, she never spent a nickel. On her horrible Grand Rapids tables, she draped this horrible barnyard plastic. Food she grubbed out of cans. She was her own dog. And this human cash register they called 'divine.' . . .

"In '30 or '31, Schulberg brought over Marlene, a fat-thighed Berlin *Bummeller* with tits like deflated footballs. I saw them, one of the few—including her so-called lovers—who did. When I made *Timbucktoo* for Lubitsch, I had the next dressing room. There was a hole in the wall and I saw her buckling these things into one of her contraptions. . . .

"Joe von Sternberg—those little Jews loved the *von*s they stuck on their names—had taught this Berlin nothing to speak, sigh, cry, dress, undress, move, sing—I should say croak—probably to fuck and suck. Though I've heard from men and women who had the not-exactly-rare privilege of her none-too-clean sheets that she had precious little interest in all that putting in and taking out; what she wanted was devotion to the shrine Sternberg had made of her.

"The only thing in the world she cared about was how she looked—on and off camera. With Sternberg's lessons, she learned the camera and how to fix herself for it. Look at her eyebrows in *The Devil Is a Woman*, those clothes in *Morocco* and *The Blue Angel*. Of course, she'd learned some of it bummelling in Berlin. Despite her Prussian airs, I'm sure she made her living in the street."

"Oh, Maman, no."

"*Mais oui, ma chèrie, absolument.*"

From Regina Delliger, *Chère Maman: A Celluloid Life*
(Harcourt Brace Jovanovich, 1984)

KENERET ★ To Work

[1]

To work.

Like a placard in his head, a newspaper headline, a gonging bell. Astonishing it wasn't in everyone else's head, Marcia's, the cook's, Mrs. Iwinaga's, his neighbor (standing by her plastic ritual bush full of baby shoes and rolled prayer tubes) not knowing—she didn't read the trades—that his alarm would ring this morning at five, the car would call for him at six, that at seven-thirty, in the early light, they'd start principal photography.

To work.

To the Paramount lot, where he hadn't been since *Billy Takes a Fall*, nineteen years ago.

Recognized. A wave. "Hcy, Mr. Keneret, good to see ya!" A grip.

Amazingly, he put a name to the lined face. "Andy, how ya doing?"

Ulysses, in Ithaca after twenty years, disguised but recognized by his old dog snoozing on the dung heap, hearing his master's voice, thumping his tail *hello* before dying. (Andy didn't die.) Directors moved on and off the lot, months, years, decades, between assignments here, but Keneret was moved, as Ulysses had been by old Argos, and, like him, concealed what it meant to him.

Getting coffee at the commissary, he saw himself, twice. Two shocks. The first was a framed caricature on the wall before the two Stans, Kramer and Kubrick: the young Keneret, wolfish grin bloodied by a recent kill. (Caricature was another cost of celebrity.) Was there truth in that savage drawing? Now and then, stories circulated back to him about the way he'd behaved on a set, outbursts, withering remarks. He'd thought of himself as quiet, courteous, concerned about everyone, tender with actors. Not with those fangs.

The second shock was seeing a bald Keneret spilling coffee into a saucer he was carrying toward a table. It looked like Grandpa Keneret. Startled, Keneret almost called to him, then saw Grandpa's mouth open, ready to call to him. Himself, in the commissary mirror. He'd turned into Grandpa.

Did Eileen see it also? Every year till he was nine, when Grandpa died, he, Eileen, and Dad went down to Grand Central to meet the old fellow with the soft silver hair and mustache getting off the *Silver Meteor* from Florida. Grandpa, his first character. Ankle-length white nightgown, hot-water bottle on his sheets, silver filigree thermos of grape juice on the bedside table, Grandpa climbing into the bed across his room. Sometimes he'd wake to his honks and snores. "Grandpa sound like choo-choo." Despite Spear's metaphysical arias about grandparenthood, there'd be no grandpas in his films, genial curmudgeons or senile ferocities. Keneret's family interests were confined to the primal pair, enough story there, at least for another millennium. Did Grandpa Keneret go to movies? Mary Pickford? Chaplin?

I'll never know now.

He did read books, magnifying glass close to the page. *The Rise of the House of Rothschild, Life of Disraeli,* lives of de Lesseps, Rathenau, Einstein, Brandeis. Keneret could see the book spines on the shelves where, after Grandpa's death, they'd stood, literary tributes to great Jews.

At Paramount, he was the closest thing to Grandpa, the oldest man in the commissary. So what? Inside, he wasn't a grandpa, wasn't a character. He was making a film. A couple of hundred people under his command were going to manufacture a few thousand feet of emulsified celluloid that would rip the breath out of a million chests all over the world. Sure.

No, he had to believe it. That's what he did, his way of being a grandpa. He was going to turn this sow's ear fetched from the middle of the Pacific into the silkiest of purses. He'd photograph her fishbone shoulders and little breasts against the chest of that puzzled kid-beauty Dillon Schorr until he could slide the story into a few million stiffened bodies. Every tremor of love and suffering would melt the job-crushed, love-and-life-starved audience, and not just for the movie's hundred minutes but, if he did it right, for months, years. They'd feel their blood connection to the ruined Europe of the forties, their lives reflected and expanded in his little narrative chip, Leet de Loor, his Gascon–Fijian–Los Angeles chippy.

Working with a studio again was being in control of great forces. The studio was the genie who summoned up what was needed. (If it also bottled you, that was the Mephistophelian contract.) There were the eighteen-wheeler panzers with miles of copper cable, enough electrical gear for a town, arcs and brutes which fought the shadows, cranes, dollies, tracks, cameras, mixers, sprinklers, generators, grids, grid cloths. And the latest stuff, Casio computers, so you could know where the sun would be any second of the year, cameras small as bread boxes, amazing sound registers (digital Nagras), electronic splicers, and montage systems. Who needed Moviolas anymore, you saw the shots as you made them. And the personnel, not his own—only Bergman, Fellini, Lucas, and Woody had their own repertory companies—but he'd been around long enough to know at least the older people, unit production managers, art directors, line producers, some of the grips and gaffers, best boys, sound mixers, boom men, wardrobe handlers, researchers, transportation coordinators, location scouts, drivers. For transport, campers, trailers, trucks, bulldozers, limousines, helicopters, whatever, submarines, comets, name it. This was no Sundance caper by the new let's-make-a-movie Andy Hardys with their handheld VCs and digital hocus-pocus. Walking past the block-long cab of an eighteen-wheeler, its insides draped with ten thousand feet of copper wire, framing picks, axes, brass bars, steel plates, Keneret felt like Patton with the pride of army command.

Was it all necessary? Perhaps, like the dark matter of the universe, an invisible density somehow indispensable to the mysterious visibility of existence. Remove one truck, one brass stud, the whole production might implode—a pretty big bang.

There was no bang. He had Paramount. And his own financier, Daniel Duggan, had worked it out, one of the complex arrangements that he rat-a-tat-tatted into Keneret's ear (though not quite into his comprehension or, for that matter, interest): "We've bought into a series of twenty-one-day units. Reversible at the conclusion of each unit. Every twenty-one days of principal photography, we show them what we have." The "them" wasn't clarified. "Limited risk. Sound all right, Ez?"

"Perfect," said Keneret.

For four years he'd been on his own, dangled in the thin air of maybe-projects, options, ideas, hopes—and then despair, terrifying despair that it was all over for him, that he'd had every chance he was ever going to get. Little consolation that he'd had—and done—more than most. It was time to fold the tent, throw in the towel, pack it up, hit the road. Which last he'd done, gone on his Harmel embassy to Australia and, by chance, come back with a Fijian lottery ticket.

[2]

Leet was on her own but, surprising herself, not frightened. After the first few weeks—during which Keneret had seen her half a dozen times and given or lent her, as she saw it, money—she got a job at a delicatessen on Wilshire Boulevard.

Talking about the transformation of her story into film did unsettle her, but Keneret told her that there was little chance it would come to anything; almost nothing came to anything out here. "Everything in the movie business is risk. As your coming here was and is."

Underneath Leet's apparent passivity, Keneret felt more puzzlement than resentment and, too, of course, loneliness. He and Marcia couldn't do much about that. When she found the job in the delicatessen, they were relieved. Less time for brooding, loneliness, resentment. Though she'd said nothing to them along those lines. At the delicatessen, she got the same sort of offer she'd gotten in Fiji, for even among the beautiful waiters and waitresses, she was special, both more remote and more down to earth. Every time he saw her rushes, he changed his mind about her. Was she actually *there,* up there, on the screen?

Her being here in California had worked on him. Guilt about his not-entirely-serious invitation to her fused with his intermittent ambition to film her and her story. One day, he roughed out the outline of an outline: *French girl leaves home after disgraced father disappears; in U.S. meets boy, maybe a soldier (Vietnam? foreign legion?), something happens; then pick up father, reunion, France, the Pacific, South America, wherever, whatever.*

When this doodling finished, he had—doodling. A bit more than nothing. Days later, energized again, he flipped through the *Writer's Guild Index,* checking names: writers he'd worked with; writers he wanted to work with.

Do I go with one who knows my kind of film or one who can write what can pull me into something new? Age shadowed him. Status shadowed him. Am I up to going through weeks, months, spelling this— whatever it is—out, selling it, tempting people, then rejecting half the tempted? Do I need this? Do I need to make this film? Any film?

On his patio, under the lemon tree, holding the *Index,* staring at the golden fruit eggs full of bittersweet juice, he said aloud, *Laggio.* Frank Laggio. He could do it. *Class of Eighty,* the film he wrote for Sydney Kleppa. A smart, oddly, finely paced story. Laggio had slowed Syd down but sharpened him. Of course they'd had that Schmitz girl. You could hardly miss with a girl like that. She'd be great for Laure. (Laure was the name he was using for the French girl.) Or would have been before her price went to twenty million. . . . Could he get her anyway?

If she knows my name, she probably thinks I made silents. Anyway, there's Leet, the real thing. She looks right, might be right. I can do it with her, give me a chance. I'll make her a Schmitz. Schmitzify her. Schmitzifaction. Hell, Keneretize her. I've done it for thirty-five years. The Keneret touch, good as gold, good as ever.

[3]

"Frank, Ez Keneret. Mutual. Absolutely, 's why I'm calling. No, I've got something myself, rough, but, in its way, complete. Who you with? No, still William Morris. Can we talk? The soonest. A week? How 'bout Sunday? Wanna come here? Santa Monica. That's right. There'll be nobody checking us out but the finches. Park on the street, no trouble."

[4]

Laggio drove a six-year-old black-and-silver Audi. Good, thought Keneret, watching it from the window. Not gaudy, likes machinery, gets his money's worth. Denims, sneakers, tennis shirt, older looking than Keneret thought he should be, white streaks in black hair, a forehead like a dry riverbed. Forty, he looked fifty. Good. A thinker. Or does he have a habit? Keneret remembered when drugs took over the studios and Hollywood nearly fell into the sewer. No, he's worked steadily, must be reliable, must be in shape. Just tired. Laggio's features bunched around a sharp nose: small black eyes, thick black-and-silver eyebrows, attentive ears. A ferret. And those lines. *You must learn your lines.* He has.

I can work with him.

Laggio sat in what Keneret called Spear's chair. Deep, leather cushioned. Every part of him listened. He didn't look at Keneret, just took in—those ears—what he said, the story, and the story of the story, how Keneret had stopped off in Fiji, found Leet in a resort, a French grace note in the Pacific; the enchantment, the puzzlement.

"Speaks beautiful, odd English."

"You want the father big?" asked Laggio.

"My feeling is three time shifts, the father when he's the girl's age, the girl in the Pacific because of what the father did, then here in L.A. with the boy from Vietnam. Unless we make it Korea or the foreign legion. There's always a good war. See how we feel with the periods. The father can turn up, if needed, to make trouble, to resolve it, whatever."

"Many possibilities."

"No reins. Feel free."

"Freedom's tough." Laggio looked up at him from the leather cushions, the black eyes probative.

He thinks I'm over the hill. "Look, Frank, you know lots of pictures start with less than this. A feeling, an idea, a face, a scene—even a sound, a rhythm."

"The question is, What am I responding to? Where am I going?"

"I'll try and show you," said Keneret. Then he made his offer. "Okay?"

"Has to be. I'm into something. Financial." Christ. That's where those lines are from; the son of a bitch is being shylocked. "Under control," said Laggio. "I keep a tight rein. I work hard."

"I hear that."

"With luck I'll have something in three, four days. That is, I'll have two places it can go, a treatment for each. And I'll do it at WGA minimum."

"If I were Spielberg, it'd be the moon. Just show me where it's going and how to get there."

[5]

Wendell Spear found a cinematographer for him: "Frydman Lukes."

"He's alive?" said Keneret.

"Like me. People aren't sure if we're alive or dead. I ran into him in Cienega Films and Books."

"Isn't he retired?"

"He's writing a history of cinematography."

"So he's finished."

"Thanks," said the film historian.

"How old is he?"

"Three years older than we are. He was nineteen when he worked with Mamoulian."

"Wendell, he has to be able to see."

"With cataracts he'd be better than half the geniuses shooting now. He learned from chaps who did color with eight ASA. Ever see *Becky Sharp?* Those reds and greens. Lukes is on the front line. If he's writing a history, it means he's keeping up. Two, three years ago, he ran a seminar at UCLA. The whole ASC crowd sat in on it, Nykvist, Willis, Storaro, Rotuno, Wexler."

"I can't raise money on the Pyramids."

"Can you afford anybody that isn't either thirteen years old or retired? Give Lukes a chance. A call. He lives on one of those ABC streets off the San Diego Freeway near Westwood. You're made for each other."

"Thanks."

"You're in the same boat."

"Worse than I thought."

"Senior cits who know films—and can still make them."

"Thank you."

"Different pace, maybe, but millions love it."

"Does he want to work?"

"Even carrying that stack of books, he was explaining how Woody mucks up black and white."

[6]

Lukes lived in a white ranch house with a curled iron lamppost and flower beds. In the back, an orange tree shaded a small flagstone terrace. He had a long Amerindian face, the nose descending with haughty rigor. There was a peculiar bareness in him, like a knothole in a tree, but the eyes—Keneret gave them a lot of attention—had none of the liquid diffuseness of the old. The hair, too, was vigorous, a surge of black waves over a small, furrowed brow. If he's dyeing his hair, he thought, he still wants in. Unless it's for women. But no, it wasn't dyed; there was plenty of silver there.

They drank tea. "Bewley's, number three. I've drunk it since I worked for Grierson. Wasn't the only thing I got from him." A soft rough voice. Not much used, a loner? Or was it from acid reflux, crud scraped out of the throat every few months? How many other leaks in this ship?

"I want to try these new emulsions, Kodak 5293, 5247. Artificial tungsten light, the meter at two hundred ASA. Gives you an extra stop when you force the negative. Who's your gaffer? Or do you want me to find one?" How long had Lukes squatted under this tree, his back to the sun, waiting? "They've forgotten how to light the way the silents did, everything reflected off ceilings. I know two gaffers who'd go along for scale. Guy Chen. You know him? Worked with Zygmond. Taught me how to take readings on the palm. Everything's so pretty through the lens, it fools you. These young guys use too much light. They come in with filters, diffusers, gauzes, meters, they want a battalion of electricians and grips. Justifies their salary; the union loves them. Chen's a great backlighter; he reads the script, always justifies the source, knows where the sun shines, knows the refractions. He worked at Centro Sperimentale in Rome, said it was like Bellini's workshop in the Quattrocento."

The Bellini hooked Keneret; they could work together. He himself had a fair eye but had never mastered the camera. His vocabulary was basic: horizontal, *peace*; vertical, *strength*; diagonal, *action*; curves, *sensuality*. He knew rhythm, two-shot, medium, long, medium, close-up, two-shot, but less about lighting than many actors. "Chen sounds good, you want to ring him?"

"What time frame we talking?" The Indian was holding back.

"That's the rub. We've got to raise money."

"Can't help you there. But my dance card isn't full. Let me have a script, I'll start."

"The moment we get it, you do."

"I see. Well, that's all right. I'm a good waiter."

Lukes walked him to his Porsche. "You've made at least four good films."

Keneret, stabbed and pleased at once, held back from asking *Which ones?*

"I may have missed a few."

[7]

Spear, who was getting as excited about the film as Keneret—although he hadn't yet thought of his book about Keneret's films—also suggested its composer. "Stanley Oxenhandler. You know he's first-rate, yet since he did that score for Harvey Altkorn, he's fallen by the wayside. It may be his size: this thin-mad crowd thinks anyone ten pounds overweight will drop dead on them."

Oxenhandler was not a promising sight nor, for that matter, sound. A coin jiggler, grunter, foot tapper, panter, heaver; a one-man band of non-music in a savanna of flesh, grassed over by a triple-extra-large stoplight-green Lacoste shirt.

While Keneret explained his idea for the score, Oxenhandler's sneak-

ers beat time to some occult rhythm. Keneret detested physical tics—
They mean no self-control, he thought—but managed not to tell him to
keep still. (Neurotic Beethoven he would have booted out the door.)

When Oxenhandler talked, the sneakers stilled. His lyric basso was the
voice of a mountain, full of peaks and dips, somewhere between speech
and music. Even pianissimo, it filled the study and—at least they were
still—apparently mesmerized the finches and jays. Saint Francis of Lipidia.

"You know, maybe you don't, I worked for John Green," sang/said Oxenhandler. "He copied *An American in Paris* for Gershwin, told me he
was a compulsive doubler because—back then anyway—he didn't know
the orchestra. He doubled violas, basses, double bassoons. John taught
him how to transpose for B-flat clarinets. Me he made learn—at least try
out—every single instrument. Only way you can score. I mean mus-
ically," and the mountain rumbled a bit.

"I loved what you did in *Local People*, those wavery, what were they,
clarinets?"

Many pounds smiled, a sky of delight. "Alto saxes with Huey reeds.
Harvey wanted ghostly stuff. I figure you want a sort of *Butterfly* shadow
for the girl plus a whiff of *South Pacific*, only rockier."

"I'd like—original, distinctive. Lukes's camera will be angular, off center, as if we're just missing what's going on. Like that."

Huge arms flew up like flamingo wings, the hands strangely graceful
as they swept close to Keneret's autographed pictures of Grant, Cooper,
Ford, Lubitsch. "I love it, Ezra."

"It's a Hawks kind of story, girl breaking into a male group, strong, sexual, sparring lovers. Then, as she learns what's going on, she turns the tables. And may disappear."

"I'll fade her with the most gorgeous whimper you ever heard." Gourds
of flesh heaved.

When this mountain copulates, Southern California must go on quake
alert.

[8]

Zemanski, a film editor, had carved a niche for himself by taking every
available job. Thick shouldered, powerful, furious, comic about un-

touchable subjects: "Hollywood Jews, studio bitches, faggots, Micks, hicks, slanteyes, spades." In southwest Chicago, he'd been adopted by a Jewish couple who ran a school for blind boys. The boys unscrewed lightbulbs and beat him up, challenged him to backward races, tripped and kicked him. After high school, he took off for California. Delivering pizza, he met, amused, insulted, and, a year later, married a department store heiress, and on her money went to film school, got a job as a cutter. Now he lived in Brentwood, read the *National Review,* loved Rush Limbaugh, and hated liberals. Hatred became him—"It's the only way I feel serious"—but he learned to conceal, even counter, it. To the powerful, he sucked up. He put his arms around Keneret, called him "dear friend," yet, making points, poked his chest. (His touching was aggressive, erotic.) He could also be gentle and affectionate, though even then his little gray eyes glinted with malice. When affection and rage fused, he looked like a pig stunned by a hammer.

Never sure of himself, Zemanski pretended to know what was going on, but it was years before he could edit on his own. Hanging around good editors, he became a fair one. About this, though, he was surprisingly modest. He surrounded himself with first-rate assistants but always feared that his ignorance and uncertainty would be outed.

Zemanski knew that Keneret saw through him. Which meant that, to some degree, Keneret could control him. When Keneret had had enough of Zemanski's rant about the *Jew York Times,* Beverly Hills knee jerks, and multicultural cocksuckers, he'd say, "Remember how you screwed up *The Girl on Rosehill Road,* Leo?" Zemanski would redden, retreat, shut up, and take off, though the next day he was back in the commissary embracing Keneret. "Dear friend, what a genius you are."

When Spear proposed Zemanski as his editor, Keneret said, "You must be nuts."

"His wife will put in money."

"She knows I see through him."

"What's there to see? He's competent, cheap, he gets good people around him, and Mrs. Z has buckets of dough."

"They're promise breakers, liars who don't even know they are."

Yet that night Keneret thought, I can scare him. He won't back out, he'll work hard. And any non-Duggan money I can pick up is insurance.

[9]

Keneret watched Simeon Slobos talking to the dashboard of his Lexus. *Rolling his calls,* they called it. Dressed by Cesare Rhett, hair by Julian, the works, but vintage 1980. Good that he's out-of-date. More respect for us antiques.

Slobos had been a packager at ICM, a residual specialist at CAA. Now partnered with an ex-wife and her ex-boyfriend, he specialized in cable rights.

Keneret watched him dismount from the tender leather, a pretty fellow with a flat auburn mustache. "Groucho meets Natalie Wood" was his description in a Bella Bigger's column. A refined little nose sniffed the neighborhood. He checked his Rolex (heavy on a slender wrist) and caught Keneret eyeing him.

The dozen different mineral waters and the wall of signed photos— Schary, Cary, Gary, Sophia, Liz and Lauren, Eisenhower, Reagan, George Murphy, and the Browns, father and son—compensated for the louche simplicity of the Keneret house and garden. Or so Keneret read the Slobos look.

"Charming house," Slobos said. "Only geniuses live like this."

"Like what?" Slobos turned up his palms, then tossed them toward terrace and honeysuckle screen. "I must introduce you to my neighbors."

"Only one genius to a block."

"Thank you, Simeon. This genius needs help." Keneret pointed to the soldierly row of mineral waters.

"Not now." Slobos sat in Spear's chair under the photographs.

Keneret, behind his desk, opened his palms, "You know what I want, Si."

"I'll get right to it, if I may. We supply our stations with *beaucoup* junk. Twelve—out of sixty-two!—use quality movies, that's four thousand hours a year, of which each reshowable ninety-minute film supplies fourteen, maybe sixteen, hours. Could be two hours and out. Eight's the average. I won't give you our gross."

Homo spreadsheetus. Said Keneret in his own business manner, "I'm not going to give you 'I've been out here forty years,' Si. You're out here, what? A dozen, and you know the ropes better than I ever will. I have a thousand-piece puzzle. You're maybe fifty pieces—crucial pieces—of it. Without you, I could lose two, three hundred other pieces. With you, our comfort zone is twenty, thirty percent wider. Banks, videos, theaters—if they're still around when we finish this—distributors. I want you in on the ground floor. You know I can make a picture, and I've got solid people who can also make them. Frydman Lukes, best cinematographer since Almendros, Guy Chen, Frank Laggio, Stan Oxenhandler, Leo Zemanski. Last, no, first, a backer for at least the first unit, Dan—

"I know that Duggan's in. Why me, then?"

"Twenty-one-day units. That's the sword he holds over me. You'd help show him—and me—that I can go without him. If I have to."

"But you can't."

"I'll feel very, very good if you're in." Keneret passed two sheets of paper over the desk. "Here you are. Actors, crew, the works. Those in blue are available, those in red we have to go after."

"You're readier than I thought you'd be."

"I wouldn't waste your time, Si. And you didn't drive out here to get my autograph."

Simeon's prettiness was gone; he looked like a knife. "*Lianne* is one of the films of my life, and I loved *Outside In* almost as much. At your—can I say weakest?—you're compelling. I am a Keneret fan. But we only have a small pot of risk money. My people—six of them—have to be for you too, and they need more than my enthusiasm."

"Any developments, you'll know as soon as I do."

A shy smile. "I might know sooner." He was up, once more the pretty fellow with the delicate auburn mustache. "You'll hear from me in seven days. I don't say 'working days.' Unlike our Maker, we don't take Sunday off. All right? I don't think you could expect more."

"Not from my mother," said Keneret.

[10]

That night, lying in bed, a foot from Marcia, Keneret thought, I can't do it. It was one thing to have an idea—he had fifty a week—and to talk it out with writers, cameramen, composers, editors, and backers, but to buckle down and do it, to make the five hundred daily decisions about everything under the movie sun with the financial bit in his mouth and the time reins on his flank, flailed by executive whips, and to do it day after day after day, while his nights were heavy with plans for tomorrow and fear about yesterday, that was something else. No wonder they don't trust old men.

"My logo reads HAS BEEN," he'd said to Spear. "If I was ever a *been*."

"You were. You are." Behind the fortress of his cigar, his tumbler of Chivas Regal, and, strongest battlement of all, his *hors de combatism*, Spear was there for him in these weeks of self-doubt.

"*You* see what *you* see, Wendell, and don't think it doesn't count for me, but they don't see me like that. They see a rocking chair, old trophies, lousy spreadsheets, and"—throwing his hand up at the wall of autographed photos—"this debris."

"I've lived with your nerves for thirty years, Ez. You're farther along on this picture than you've been with half the others."

"I'm in a tornado: fee structures, completion bonds, first money, crew, guilds. I dream I'm on location, eighteen-wheelers, wires, cables, scaffolds, a thousand people, and I'm in the middle, the crew, the actors, waiting; and I can't move, there's nothing to shoot." Gray smoke—there was no relief from it for Spear's friends—poured from the cigar. "I can't remember feeling like this."

They went outside, Keneret seeking relief from the smoke.

Spear said, "Pretend you're just starting out. Nothing to prove. You just want to shoot your film. Scratch something here, something'll come up there. I remember when Bobby Townsend bought raw stock with credit cards, stole locations, never told the police about them, the crew wore UCLA T-shirts. He produced a rough cut for eighty thousand dollars, then walked it into every distributor's office himself, gave it to the secretaries, who told their bosses about it. He screwed in the lightbulbs, swept the floors, made the coffee himself."

"And was thirty years old. Then what happened? What did he do for posters, blowups, ads, shipping, promo tours, screenings? Are you kidding? Wendell, this isn't kindergarten, you need—"

"He worked it out, as you will: everything under deferment, distribution fees taken off the top, limited partners—"

"Find me some."

"—dollar-for-dollar shares with general partners. No cross-collateralization by the distributor against other markets, downside protection from cable, video—"

"Enough. This isn't helping. I can't face it."

"Sure you can. It was make or break for Bobby. You're already you, you've got thirty-five years of wonderful work in the can. If this doesn't make it, you still have it. What's the worst that can happen?"

Humiliation, defeat, exhaustion, emptiness, death. Wendell had taken off for the hills twenty-five years ago, turned into scenery. Okay for him, not me. "I could lose months, years, my shirt, other people's shirts. Plus going out a bum. Staining the record you say I have. Even if it all worked out, even if I made a good picture, it could be a disaster, no one coming, no one liking it. Remember *The Unmaking of Janie?*"

"A wonderful picture. I don't care what happened."

"I thought everything was perfect. Principal photography in forty days, tryout cards sensational, great reviews—you wrote the best one—full-page ads, TV spots. And? Second week's gross, zero. Nothing. No word of mouth. No good word. Seattle, Philly, New York, Chicago, Houston. Nothing."

"But it was made, it exists, a beautiful film. I read a piece about it last year."

"Even saints have a failure quota. I've filled mine." He poured more scotch into Spear's glass. "Here I am, talking as if this one's going to get off the ground."

[11]

Laggio's treatments were terrible.

Dear Frank,

Beautiful things here, just not my things. The girl's too hard, the boy's a moron. The father has something, but it's unexplained, I can't see it.
But I'm grateful you did it so quickly.

Ez

Check enclosed.

[12]

Harmel called. "I hear Laggio blew the script."

"Wendell tell you?"

"No, he did. Look, Ez, my boys are high on a writer named Sfaxe. You know him?"

"No."

"Of course you never know with the boys." According to Marcia, salmon had more paternal feelings than Harmel. "Still, they keep up. Want them to call you?"

"Sure."

"Buy them lunch. Listen to them, but I wouldn't let them get any closer."

[13]

Keneret met the Harmel brothers, Oscar and Sylvan, at Fanciullo's.

Sylvan said, "André's a young guy, but good."

"Your generation?"

Sylvan patted the little pot under his polo shirt. Thought Keneret, These forty-year-olds look like teenagers. "Younger."

Oscar said, "He almost got a Tony nomination."

"'Almost' isn't a credit."

Sylvan: "At Sundance they said *Running and Crossing* should have won."

"I must have missed that."

Oscar: "He's a little Mamet—"

Sylvan: "Filtered through Woody."

Oscar: "Farce with a death rattle."

Keneret had watched the brothers grow up and listened for years to their father's complaints about them, but only now, here in the window booth at Fanciullo's, did he notice how much they looked like Floyd, with their sloping foreheads, black eyes, Popeye forearms. There was, though, something crucially different about them: they seemed weightless, and somehow older than their father, as if life's bad news, which he'd slowly digested with the good, was known to them even before it happened.

"How about story?" he asked them. "Sfaxe talk about that?"

A waiter, a young Nick Nolte, blond and rugged, appeared with an aria about the specials.

Oscar, imperious, sliced it off. "Linguini here. Syl, the same?" He held up two fingers. "Ez?"

"An Ovitzburger."

Oscar waved off the waiter. "André breathes and eats story."

Sylvan: "He's special, Ez. We wouldn't sell you a lemon."

"I know, boys." *Boys*, he thought, forty-year-old boys. Yet he knew they cared for him, especially Sylvan, who'd talked of making a documentary about his films, another one of the projects which, said his father, added up to the Great Zero of their accomplishments. "Is André French?"

"Like Nebraska," said Sylvan.

"Right. How did you find him?"

Oscar: "Santa Anita. He lives in Pasadena, goes out a few times a week. Syl and I bought a two-year-old in a claiming race, so we go out every week. We run into him."

Sylvan: "He knows nags. He coins it out there."

Keneret: "Nice credential: the Trifecta King."

"He could live off it," said Oscar. "I've never seen a smarter picker. Last week, he took them for thirty K."

Sylvan: "We're talking genius, Ez."

[14]

Two days later, in the same booth, Keneret sat with André Sfaxe, as unwriterly a writer as he'd ever seen. Keneret had a Lamarckian sense that people in the same line of work had similar stigmata, the irregular shoulders of laborers, the bunched necks of miners and submariners, the swollen fingers of tailors and cobblers. Writers should look alert and either eager or laid back. The bald fellow across the table looked like a rag doll, something hastily assembled and rushed onstage, lines unlearned. "Oscar and Sylvan think a lot of you." Silence. "Mind telling me something about yourself?"

"Yes."

"I understand that." Keneret drank up the Chablis and pointed young Nolte to the glass. "It's just that I have a problem. I'm supposed to sell people on a project, and I need a script for it. Even a treatment. Oscar and Sylvan said they outlined the story for you. Are you interested? I mean, you're here. Want to know more about it?"

The ostrich egg bent, the eyes, very light blue, caught light and almost vanished. Keneret had doffed his eyeglasses to eat and drink, and anything two feet away blurred. Sfaxe looked like a puff of smoke.

"Not necessary. I've got it." The puff tapped itself. "Abstract."

Keneret forked up linguini and held it aloft. "Like Rothko? Mondrian?"

"The abstract. The essence!"

"It's basically a strong story. A real audience story: father, daughter, abandonment, old wounds, new starts, boy and girl."

"I don't dis audience."

"I sense you're not comfortable with this member of it."

Sfaxe put his fork into a shrimp, held it up like a specimen. "I've seen *Lianne* four times."

If Griffith himself had hung a medal about his neck, Keneret would not have been more delighted. He raised the wineglass to cover the smile he couldn't suppress. "Was it that good?"

"Yes."

"Now that you mention it, I think this story is similar."

"The tension-release-tension of *Lianne* is similar."

"Strong girl, hesitant boy, different sides of the tracks."

"No," said Sfaxe. "The bliss of the void."

Keneret waited. "Oh." He drank and signaled young Nolte to refill. "I hadn't thought of that. Might be hard to film."

Sfaxe was more at ease in silence than he. He ate a shrimp, sliced a tomato, sipped his tea, and looked peacefully, whitely, at Keneret, who was about to throw in the towel when he heard, "You'll have a treatment by Friday."

Keneret put down his wineglass, put on his eyeglasses, and looked hard across the table. "André, I have a feeling I'm going to love it."

Some clients wait to be picked. You flick the stem with your finger, off they come. Bums and no-counts can have those clients.

We fetch our clients, we kidnap them, cut them out of wombs. That means work, research, smarts. We have to know wants, fears. We have to know the instant "X" gets a part, so we can call "Y." "X got your part. Come to us, that won't happen." "A" makes a deal; if "B" makes a better deal, "A" is threatened. We call him: he's ours.

. . . Nothing is new. Every event is other events. Everything has history. You can work for years before you crack a big client. Flowers, sympathy notes, a Rolex, "token of appreciation." For the way you handled that scene with Michelle. Better than Davis in *Jezebel*, than Rainer in *Ziegfeld*. We give them historic grandeur, and they're ours . . .

. . . I put a million dollars into this office. In the old office, I wouldn't meet with our own agents. It stank of failure. You come here, there's excitement; you haven't seen anything like this. "Is it a window or a painting?" "Is that a mirror? Man, I look great here." Fragrance. Texture. Fruit. It's paradise. It's promise. It's yours—if you're mine.

From Gerry M. Nuklis,
Slash: An Agent's Story (Dutton, 1992)

SPEAR ⋆ Audited

[1]

Spear did not think of himself as an avaricious man. Lord knows he could be generous, easily to his granddaughter, Jennifer, and, under pressure of his superego, to causes. It was just that after the death of his wife and the consequent, though still baffling, estrangement from Amelia, Jennifer's mother, money became a sort of companion to him, or, sometimes, more child than his child. The nurture and growth of his modest fortune brought him both tension and ease and, though he knew this was absurd, if not shameful and vulgar, pride.

Every morning, a minute or two after waking, he pressed the memory buttons on the bedside phone which summoned the electronic voices which reported the status of his brokerage accounts and mutual funds. Now and then, a glitch in the reporting system filled him with anxiety and fury until he reached a live voice which assured him that, no, there had been no overnight embezzlement of his holdings.

When, in August, a letter from the Treasury Department informed him that he was subject to a tax audit, he felt a terror unlike anything he'd known since Vanessa's death. Why, after all the placid, solitary years in his Malibu Canyon cabin, had he been singled out?

The letter was personalized to the extent of specifying the year the IRS was auditing and the areas of its concern, his contributions and business expenses. It also indicated the place and time of the audit—the Federal Office Building on Los Angeles Street—and the auditor's sinisterly comic name, G. Whipp.

Spear's longtime accountant, Zack Wool, filed his returns from Los Angeles, where Spear had lived till his move to Malibu. This accounted for the location of the audit and another dimension of his anxiety—the hour's drive on the freeways. The freeways were the incarnation, the impetrification, of his fears, stone arteries clogged with the life-killing busyness which, years ago, he'd fled.

He called Wool's office. Frances, Wool's administrative assistant, said, "I'm sorry, Mr. Spear. He's in South America."

"In flight?"

"Vacation. Remember he takes September off."

"It's August."

"He'll be back September twentieth."

"The audit's September eighteenth."

"I can go with you, or I can request a postponement. They're good about granting them."

"I may not last till September eighteenth. Thank you, Frances, I'll handle it myself."

"That might be best. Mr. Wool has been known to put auditors to sleep." Frances was not averse to chaff about her number-besotted employer. ("Dull as his name," Keneret told him when, thirty years ago, he'd introduced him to Spear. "But he doesn't pull it over your eyes.")

"I probably should wait for him; but I can't: the waiting would do me in."

[2]

That afternoon Spear dug out of a closet the manila envelopes which held the tax forms, checks, receipts, bankbooks, Visa, and American Express bills, and went to work.

After two hours' immersion, he went out to the terrace from whose eaves still hung the inverted blue bottles which, so long ago, Vanessa and Amelia had filled with sugar water for hummingbirds. (The birds had departed with them.) Looking over the small lawn bordered with chaparral, palm, and cypress, he prepared himself for the actual hearing. He'd wear his oldest decent suit, blue, a frayed blue shirt, and faded blue tie. No, wrong look: too much blue. Too much attention to color coordination. The artist disguises his art; the con man also. He needed a shirt that clashed, not enough to agitate a color-sensitive auditor but enough to suggest an old widower, careful but a bit at sea. Maybe a white shirt with black stripes. Whoops: prison colors. The lemon green then with a few honorable loose threads at the collar. For shoes, the ugly, broad-toed ones with worn-down heels. He'd polish them to show how careful he was with his old, unfashionable things. Whipp would see a decent, even fastidious, man, straightforward, plain, a not-quite-with-it man, a bald, sexagenarian widower, honorable son of an honorable, impoverished Anglican clergyman, keeping up as well as he could in this still-alien—after decades—corn.

Would the auditor sniff something askew? After all, he knew Spear's income, tiny compared with many in Malibu but probably three times bigger than his own. *I'm saving for my granddaughter, Mr. Whipp. I'm no spender. I skimp, but never on taxes. I pay what I owe. My accountant, Zack Wool, is descended from a Confederate general in your Civil War. He's stricter than a ruler. I'm sure he makes me pay more than I should. I'm expecting a refund.*

Spear went back to his checks, receipts, and business expenses, including the secretarial money paid to Leet de Loor who'd helped him with his book on Ez Keneret's films after the collapse of her own. There were charities, almost thirty of them, to some of which—thinking ahead to just such an encounter—he'd given ten dollars or less. The more checks, the more scrupulous the taxpayer, the wearier the auditor. There were, though, several unusual deductions, the biggest the gift of his filmography to Claremont College. Wool had also allowed him to take the appraiser's bill as a deduction. The appraiser—*Deirdre Seale, Mr. Whipp, a well-respected professional*—had evaluated the gift at $19,650. Was this the nail on which the IRS wanted to hang him? He got out a copy of Ms.

Seale's letter, a two-page account of her credentials and a five-page detailed description of the gift. Detailed, yes, but impregnable? Perhaps Ms. Seale had left a trail of overassessments which the omniscient Whipp followed.

Omniscient?

Who knew what Whipp knew? The myrmidons of the IRS had immense resources, terrifying power. About money, they might know everything—more than everything! Spear had heard a hundred horror stories: people, companies, studios tied up in decades of litigation, tax penalties mounting at each stage of appeal.

Beyond appeal, beyond litigation, beyond impoverishment, loomed prison.

Spear knew prisons. He'd seen Jimmy Cagney, George Raft, Humphrey Bogart, Burt Lancaster, and a hundred others behind iron bars; had seen brutal wardens—Hume Cronyn the worst—and guards with guns ready, willing and eager to shoot prisoners momentarily diverting themselves from sticking cell-made shivs into each others's flanks. Gangs, extortion, sodomitic rape. Could a man like himself last a day in such a place? Three years ago, Roger Kobble, the grandson of his friend Alice, the manager of the Mobil station on Highway 1, had been sent away for six months: reckless driving and endangerment. Said Alice, "It turned him around, Mr. S. Fellow in the next cell, a stockbroker, put him onto books. Now he talks of nothing but learning the Latin language. I was happy, I thought it meant he wanted to be a priest. But no, it was just something the broker suggested. Could that help him invest? Not that he'll have anything to invest at this rate." Roger, a giant with oil-stained fingers, had grown up in the service station, not, like Spear, in an English rectory filled with the Latin classics Roger apparently craved. (Although he hadn't looked at them for years, Spear still owned the twenty-six green and gold volumes of the Loeb Library Classics left him by his father.) A minimum-security prison with three squares a day and a stockbroker companion was a step up for Roger, but for Spear, who lived in the ease of self-pampered solitude, it would be living death.

[3]

The IRS district office was on the twelfth floor of the old Federal Office Building. For his 9:00 A.M. appointment, Spear was on the Santa Monica Freeway at 7:00 A.M. and on Los Angeles Street at 8:15. Carrying his schoolboy's briefcase stuffed with rubber-banded papers, he walked around the block to compose himself.

On the twelfth floor, he gave his name to an already-weary black woman who told him to "sit in reception," a bleak room with three rows of blue plastic chairs that bespoke a harsh if not demonic thrift. The windows were so begrimed that Spear did not bother trying to see what could have been a fine view west over the city to the Pacific.

An elderly black man sat two seats away. "Mornin'," he said. He wore lavender slacks and a Hawaiian sport shirt; no blue suit and frayed shirt for him. This was Southern California; not even funeral directors wore blue suits.

"Good morning."

"Bein' audited?"

"I'm afraid so."

"They want twenny-five hunnert from me."

"Goodness me."

"My missus's cousin lifted my 'curity card, went round Arizony hangin' paper on it." He tapped a vinyl briefcase. "Got me coupla his checks."

"Looks like you're home free then."

"Think so?"

"I do," said Counselor Spear.

"Mr. McKeeney?" A stout Chinese-American woman in a glitter pantsuit stood in the doorway.

"Here I be," said the man. "And here I goes."

Spear watched him disappear round an L leg of corridor. The elevator nearby discharged a wheelchair which rolled toward reception. Spear looked at then away from its occupant, a tiny white man in a brown corduroy workshirt and blue pants from which hung tiny shoes. Not enough that God's afflicted the poor fellow, the IRS has to pursue him. Then he heard what was surely his name, "Mr. Thpear," spoken in a sharp, high-pitched voice.

Spear looked at the wheelchair. "Mr. Whipp?"

The man had an almost-normal-sized head jammed, neckless, onto small shoulders. "Pleathe follow me."

Spear rose, his seventy inches heavy with normality, and followed the wheeled throne of his auditor down the corridor into a cubicle. Whipp pointed to a wooden chair, then wheeled himself behind the desk. On a table to his left were a telephone, a small American flag on a stand, and a six-inch plastic Venus de Milo.

"Well, Mr. Thpear," he said with a pleasant smile, "thall we begin?"

"I guess I'm ready."

Whipp opened a manila envelope. "I'm going to wead you your wighth."

The familiar phrase, even in Whipp's infantile phonemes, coiled around Spear's contracted heart. "You thould have copieth of thith." Spear nodded. "In thwee or four weekth, I'll mail you a weport. If you don't agwee wiv it, you can call me or my thupervithor. If we don't thatithfy you, you can appeal. If—"

"Yes, I did read that, Mr. Whipp."

"Have you ever been audited before?"

"No."

Whipp drew a paper from the folder and said, kindly, "It theemth you were—back in 1968."

"Really?" Vanessa had done their taxes, but yes, he remembered something. An auditor had come to their house in Beverly Glen. "My wife handled our finances. I'm a widower now."

"I thee." This was not an expression of sympathy. Whipp was looking at papers which specified the date of Vanessa's death. "Now I will wead you a litht of thingth. Would you pleathe anthwer yeth or no to each? Have you any income from weal ethtate?"

"No."

"Overtheath invethtmenth?"

"Only the royalties described in the return."

"Dwug dealing?"

"No."

"Mining?"

"No."

"Cuwenthy twanthacthionth?"

"No. I don't speculate. Except for the investments listed."

At each of Spear's answers, Whipp checked off a box; then he put the paper on a pile and pulled out a pad of yellow paper. "Thall we begin with contwibutionth?"

Spear undid the leather thongs of his bricfcasc and withdrew the envelope in which he'd put charitable checks, receipts, and acknowledgments.

Whipp said, "There ith the matter of the car you donated to the half-way houthe." For years, Spear, following a tip from Keneret, had given his old cars to an ex-actor who ran a halfway house for ex-prisoners and ex-addicts. The actor tuned up the cars, then sold them to support the house. "I think the appwaithal ith too high."

"It's their appraisal, not mine."

"I think it'th too high. Do you know the Blue Book appwaithal of an eighty-thwee Buick?"

"No."

"I'll look it up. I think we have to go by that."

"It had an exceptionally good stereo system," lied Spear.

"It ith hard to appwaith thingth. Do you have any wetheith for the thound thythtem?"

"Receipts? I p-p-robably did," said Spear. "But I don't think I can f-f-find them."

"I thee." Whipp wrote on the lined pad. "We'd better uthe the Blue Book." He looked up as if awaiting Spear's approval. Spear nodded. Curled over the pad, Whipp wrote, tiny fist encircling the pen as if writing required every bit of his strength and concentration. "Now we thould look at the donathon of the—thith ith a new word to me—film-o-gwaphy." The accent was on "graph." "To the colledth libwary."

Spear said, "I have the appraiser's letters and the Claremont librarian's thank-you note here."

"Your accountant thubmitted copieth."

"Is there a problem?"

"Ith a film-o-gwaphy movieth?"

"Mine's a detailed, alphabetized description of films, categorized by genre."

"What is genwe?"

"Type of film. Comedy, tragedy. Whatever."

"I thee." Whipp's neckless head bobbed in appreciative comprehension. "I think we can acthept thith appwaithal."

"Good," said Spear, surprised at the depth of his relief.

Whipp wrote several more lines, then looked up. "Chawitieth? You have lotth of thmall oneth, and then mithellaneouth. Of courth, people can't document evwything. Like you go to church and put a few dollarth in the plate."

"That's right," said Spear, who hadn't been to church since, fifty-odd years ago, he'd endured his father's tormented sermons.

Item by item, the examination continued, Whipp writing away, Spear occasionally contesting, Whipp nodding, agreeing, asking for documentation. "The IREth won't acthept undocumented twanthacthionth."

"I understand. I wish I'd kept everything."

"I know that'th hard to do. But that'th all we have to go by. The checkth you gave thith thecwetawy, Mith de Loor—pwetty name—I can acthept, but not the cath money you thay you gave her for mithellaneouth editorwial work. Though I perthonally believe you did."

"Thank you. I appreciate that."

"And you have the woyalty thtatement againtht which the paymenth can be counted."

"It is a relief when things tally up like that." Spear wanted to tell Whipp what a small part this tally was of the hundreds of hours' writing, dictating, talking out, correcting, and analyzing Keneret's films. If memory was a shadow, these numbers were shadows of shadows, souvenirs of souvenirs.

"Yeth. For me too."

An hour, two hours, three hours, Whipp and Spear faced each other over the checks, receipts, appraisals, and assessments.

"You mutht be getting hungwy. Wouldn't it be better to make another appointment?"

"Lord no, Mr. Whipp. I'd like to get it over with now. If that's all right?"

"All wight. We're almotht finithed."

. . .

The final twenty minutes went by in a blur. Drained, Spear agreed to everything and had the impression that most of his claims were accepted. What a decent person Whipp was, and how well he dealt with his handicap. Near the end, they discussed the expenses of a trip Spear had made to a Harmel film festival in San Francisco. Whipp said, "Than Fwanthithco ith thuch a beautiful thity. I wath there oneth. Four dayth. It wath my happietht perthonal time." Spear almost reached over to pat the little hands.

[4]

The drive home on the Santa Monica Freeway and Coast Highway was actually pleasant: few cars, much relief. Home, Spear slept till wakened by the phone. "Mr. Thpear?"

"Mr. Whipp. Is anything wrong?"

"You left your bwiefcathe here."

"How careless of me."

"What thall I do with it?"

Why don't you keep it as a souvenir? Spear almost said. "I'll have to come get it."

It happened that Spear's beloved granddaughter, Jennifer Abarbanel, had been sent down from San Francisco to do a deposition at the Roybal Building across the street from the Federal Office Building. She was spending the night with Spear—a rare treat for him—and said she'd pick up the briefcase during her lunch break.

That night, she said, "The people in the office all know him. At least they've seen him in the street being carried into taxis."

"What did he say to you?"

"Not much. He was embarrassed, I think, gruffer than he might have been with you. All he said was, 'I have it wight here.' Odd speech . . . maybe because his throat's jammed into his chest."

"I'm sure he was delighted to see you. I don't imagine he gets much chance to talk to attractive girls." For Spear, Jennifer was lovelier than any film star, a taller, more solid Natalie Wood or Winona Ryder, a bit like the eighteen-year-old Hannah Arendt as she was spotted in the Marburg lecture hall by the swinish genius Martin Heidegger. (After the Leet project had fallen through, Spear suggested that Keneret try selling a movie about Arendt and Heidegger to Ryder, a Jewish girl who actually looked like the young Arendt. "It'd be too much of a stretch for her," said Keneret.) "You made his week. And probably improved my case." He decided to send Jennifer whatever refund he got.

"Doesn't he make you feel good about technology?" she said. "A few years ago, a computerless Whipp couldn't have gotten a job in a circus; they don't use cripples. He'd have been human junk."

"It's a great case for affirmative action, I suppose."

"One up for the U.S. of A.," said Jennifer.

[5]

Three weeks later, Whipp's report arrived, six pages long and so ambiguously phrased that Spear couldn't tell whether he owed money or was getting some back. There were also spelling errors and such peculiarities as credit for a safety-deposit box which Spear hadn't listed, let alone claimed. The upshot, though, was that Whipp disagreed with much of what Spear thought he'd agreed to, and Spear owed thirty-four hundred dollars, including two years' interest. It was not a great sum of money for him, and by agreeing to accept the assessment, that would end it, but something held him back. He felt that his new friend wasn't such a friend after all, and this made him both angry and sad. It also occurred to him that if he agreed to Whipp's refusal to recognize, say, the tax deductibility of a film festival, then other Whipps could question other returns, past and future. The thirty-four hundred dollars could be the first of many installments.

He called Zack Wool. "How was Machu Picchu?"

"They keep it up very nicely. What can I do you for, Wendell? How was the audit? Sorry I wasn't there. I'm sure you handled it well. Plus, if I'd gone, it would have cost you."

"I thought it went all right, until I got the report just now. The chappie went back on everything I assumed he'd agreed to. I owe thirty-four hundred dollars. Not a fortune—"

"If you don't owe it, it's thirty-four hundred too much."

"It's the business of questioning my way of life. If I'd been buying and selling hardware instead of watching movies, he would have accepted everything without question. My business is seeing films. If it looks like fun, let him try writing about them. Incidentally, he's a crippled dwarf, in a wheelchair. I actually liked him. I'm hurt he turned his back on me. I don't know what to do."

"Appeal."

"Is it worth it?"

"Is your time so valuable?"

"My leisure's valuable."

"Is it worth seventeen hundred dollars an hour? It'll only take a couple of hours."

"Plus the ride from Malibu."

"If we win, that's deductible."

[6]

Wool had spent the weekend in Santa Barbara—a surprise to Spear who subconsciously assumed that Wool never left the office—and said he'd pick up Spear at his cabin.

"Make it the Mobil station on the highway. Spare you the drive up the canyon. They know me."

The appointment with Whipp was at 1:00 P.M. Wool said he'd pick Spear up at noon, cutting it too close for Spear, who liked to be early for appointments.

He was down at the station talking to Alice Kobble at 11:30. At 11:40, he started looking up the road for Wool's car. At ten of, he said, "That damn idiot."

"What's up, Mr. Spear?" called Roger, who between stints at the gas pump was reading a Latin grammar behind the cash-register counter, clodhoppers up on two five-gallon oil cans.

"M-m-my ride's late."

"When was it supposed to be here?"

"Noon."

"It's ten of."

"*T-t-tempus* fucks us, Rog," said Spear (obscene only in moments of exasperation). A week ago, Roger had asked Spear if he'd consider giving him Latin lessons. "I haven't read Latin in years. You might as well ask me to make you an astronaut."

"I could go with that."

"Not to the moon, Roger."

He went inside to phone Wool's office. "Where's Sitting Bull, Frances? We have an appointment in L.A. at one."

"He said he'd be picking you up, Mr. Spear. He'll be there."

"Can you call his car?"

"Wish I could. He says cellular phones are carcinogenic."

"I've got a good mind to drive myself."

"Mr. Wool is sooo—deliberate. But reliable."

"What's he doing in Santa Barbara? I thought he never left L.A."

"You'll never guess. He's courting."

"Zachary G. Wool! I don't believe you."

"Last week, he asked me to pick out some sport shirts for him. I guess my mouth opened too wide. He sort of blushed, but he was proud too. It was touching. He said he was seeing this woman real-estate agent."

"Zack without a necktie—and with a woman! What are things coming to, Frances?"

"Oh, Mr. Spear, let him have fun."

"Me! Fun's the house specialty. Except when Internal Revenue has a noose around m-m-my neck. Internal Revenue! W-w-what a name, Frances. As if it's m-m-marketing your guts. I'll give him five minutes, then I'm off. He can meet me at the Federal Building. G. Whipp, twelfth floor."

"I'll tell him, sir, but please hold just a bit, I'm sure he's on his way."

Spear looked down the road, straining to pick up signs of Wool's car.

Nothing. He was backing out his Mustang when he heard something. Another surprise: Wool pulling up in a blue Lexus. At least he wasn't in one of his sport shirts.

Wool said he wanted to drop by his office to pick up Spear's file.

Suppressing the rage bursting through his anxiety, Spear said coldly, "If you didn't bring it with you, you'll have to wing it. I do not want to be late, Zack. In fact, I wish we were there now."

"Your call, Wendell."

On the Coast Highway, Wool's molasses pace had Spear clutching his head. Every time a car passed, honking to get them over to the right lane, Spear wanted to strangle him. The man shouldn't be allowed to drive a Lexus.

[7]

In the reception area, Spear, pretending to look through his papers, sat a row away from Wool. When he saw the wheelchair at the end of the corridor, he got up, opened the glass door, and greeted Whipp, who today was in tie and shirt. His shoes looked new—shiny, tiny black oxfords which hung from withered legs. "Mr. Wool. Mr. Whipp."

Wool leaned over and took Whipp's hand. "I'm the signature at the bottom of the page. You may have seen it at the bottom of other returns."

How tight the blue tie looked on Whipp's necklessness. He was balder than Spear recalled, the remnants of light brown hair like torn curtains on the sides of his head. He did seem more comfortable today, perhaps knowing that there'd be no shocked looks on a strange face. He knew that Spear would have prepared the accountant for his appearance.

"Pleathe follow me." He rolled up the corridor, going this time to a door with an alarm system whose buttons he pressed. "Could you pleathe get the door?" Spear opened it, then followed the chair left and right into Whipp's cubicle. "Thame offith," he said. There was, though, a new ornament, a pumpkin with an unlit candle inside. Had Whipp carved it himself or had some grateful client brought it in for Halloween?

"I've done a little wethearth on allowable deductionth for authorth. You are a full-time author, Mr. Thpear, aren't you?"

"I suppose so. I do sometimes lecture, but basically I am a film critic and historian."

"A hithtorian ith an author?"

"Yes."

"Mr. Spear is modest, Mr. Whipp," said Wool. "He's a very distinguished film critic and historian. He's known by and knows some of the leading film people here. Directors like my clients, Ezra Keneret and Floyd Harmel, respect him enormously."

"I do altho, Mr. Wool."

"His main business is this form of authorship."

"That'th what I thought. Therth a cathe here"—Whipp picked up a xeroxed page—"3/26/71 U.Eth.A. Dithtwict Court, Centwal Dithtwict California. I can make a copy for you. Thith man thpent thwee hundwed and thirty-five dayth in New York Thity pweparing a book on D. W. Gwiffith. I know you know who he ith. I've theen hith filmth mythelf. *Birth of a Nathon*. I'm not thure it could be thown now." He looked up as if asking for Spear's professional opinion.

"It does strain the conscience, but it is shown to film students."

"Gwiffith'th paperth were in New York, thith man lived in California. He claimed twavel and living expentheth for the taxable year. Owiginally, the claimth were dithallowed, but, on appeal, it wath dethided that the expentheth were deductible. They were not nondeductible exthpenditureth for the impwovement of a capital athet. If you'd witten a book or had wetheived an advanthe for a book about the film fethtival you attended, there would be no quethtion—bathed on thith cathe—that it wath deductible."

"But films are my business," said Spear, "whether I write about them immediately or not."

Whipp smiled his sweet smile and nodded. "I underthtand. I underthtand that it'th your bithineth to know filmth, but here'th another cathe that applieth. A high-thchool teacher of Fwench went to Fwanthe to impwove her Fwench. The court dethided that her twavel expentheth could not be deducted thinthe she wath not wequired to go to Fwanthe. It wath her choithe, her pleathure. Though she wath a Fwench teacher."

"Absurd and unfair," said Spear. "She'd give her pupils the benefit of her new knowledge of the language and the country. The only way I learned French was a year teaching in France."

Whipp opened his palms helplessly. "Yeth, I underthtand, but I can only do what the IREth allowth me to do. They would not allow me to deduct your expentheth in Than Fwanthithco unleth you had a contwact to wite about it."

Spear started to speak, but Wool touched his arm. "Our contention is that Mr. Spear's status as a film critic and historian depends upon his keeping up with what's going on in films around the world. Even in partial retirement he does that. If he doesn't do it, there will be no contracts, no invitations to write articles or books. It's not a question of not being required by an employer to go to such festivals. Mr. Spear is self-employed."

"If I don't keep up, I won't be employed at all. Don't you see, Mr. Whipp, that you're undermining my very way of life?"

Whipp shook his head. "I wethpect your way of life vewy much, Mr. Thpear. I'm thure that you are a vewy fine and important cwitic. I underthtand how important it ith for you to keep up with filmth. It'th jutht that I can't thee that your cathe ith ath clothe to the Gwiffith cathe ath it ith to the Fwench teacher'th."

"What would it take to convince you, Mr Whipp?"

The little shoulders shrugged. "I will do more wethearth and thee if I can find a cathe clother to yourth. I've had only one other author in my time here, and hith cathe wath diffwent."

"Curious. What was his name?"

Wool said, "He can't tell you that, Wendell."

"Let'th thee, you were in Than Fwanthithco fwom Febuwery eleventh to the fifteenth. Do you have thome kind of journal or diawy of that time?"

"As a matter of fact, I do. Keeping journals is part of my work."

"Vewy good." Spear handed over the notebook. Whipp looked it over, turned the pages, and handed it back. "It'th a bit hard to wead. Could you pleathe wead the entwy for, thay, Febuwery thirteenth?"

Spear took the notebook and began to read a description of his breakfast. "I'd better go to what counts."

"Pleathe."

He read a section about a 1963 Harmel film, an account of the plot along with speculations about its political and social undercurrents, the quality of the acting, the subtlety of the editing, the frames and rhythm. He read for two or three minutes till Whipp said, "That'th a vewy beautiful dethcwiption of the movie. However, there ith no hour-by-hour account of your activitieth."

"I was watching the film, Mr. Whipp."

"Yeth, I know that. But the quethtion ith what part of your day wath pleathure, what part wath impwoving your thtudieth ath a cwitic, and what part wath actually wemunewated. That ith, bithineth. That'th the difficult quethtion."

"Mr. Whipp, do you enjoy your work?"

"Yeth, I do, Mr. Thpear."

"I do too. Pleasure, then, isn't the criterion. If I were buying or selling nuts and bolts, there'd be no question about my expenses. Films are my nuts and bolts. They may sound like pleasure—they are pleasure—but they're how I earn a living. I'm not just talking about the money now, Mr. Whipp. I can afford to pay the IRS what it wants, but I can't afford to give it my life. It's my life that it's questioning. That you're questioning. The serious business of my life."

"I'm not quethtioning your bithineth, Mr. Thpear."

"I agree, Wendell. Mr. Whipp knows that you're a serious critic of films, but"—Wool turned to Whipp—"Mr. Spear has put our case well, if more emotionally, than I might."

"I underthtand that."

"All his experience goes into what he writes, and though we know that some experience—say, taking a drive or a walk—is nondeductible, going to a film festival or doing research for an article or book should be."

"I agwee with you."

"I have done this man's taxes for thirty years. I do the taxes of many film people. You've probably seen my signature. With Wendell Spear, I have no worries. He's not a person who tries to get away with anything."

Spear felt himself flushing. Of course he tried to get away with things. He was only less bold than others, more fearful of the consequences. There were drops of sweat in Wool's brow furrows. Wool was worked up. "If he does a review for a local paper and gets twenty-five dollars for it, he notes it down. He is what you call a straight arrow."

"You might thay a weal Thpear," said Whipp, smiling.

Spear smiled, too. What a little card he was. A sort of critic, too, observing the actors who performed their evasions in front of him.

"My hope is that we can resolve our problems here and now. If not . . ."

"You can appeal to my thupervithor." Whipp sounded not only sympathetic but encouraging. "And if that doethn't work, the taxth board. They may thee your cathe ath you thee it." Wide went the little palms, wide the smile. Spear surged with affection for him. If things were different, they might be friends, though Whipp's friends would have their hands full, lifting his chair and him, helping him dress, helping him in the bathroom.

[8]

Two days later, Whipp's revised examination report was in his mailbox. It was clear that no midnight oil had been burned. The only difference from the first report was that he allowed Spear two per diems at the film festival: sixty-eight dollars. Zack Wool's bill would be quadruple that. At this rate, the appeal process would bankrupt him.

Disappointed, even angry, Spear still could not bring himself to dislike the auditor. He debated calling him up to remonstrate or even plead with him to see his side of things. "You're suggesting that I don't go to festivals or do archival research since I can review films or lecture about them without going or researching. Don't you—won't you—see that the quality of the reviews and lectures will be lower? Is that what you—or the IRS—want to do, lower the quality of a person's work? It almost makes someone like me"—Spear was talking out loud to the palms and cypress—"an old-fashioned liberal, an admirer of Attlee and Harold Wilson, FDR and Harry Truman, want to side with Tories and Republicans." If the palms, so disdainful against the blue sky, said anything, it was *Pay the two dollars*.

Spear took the mail into his study, signed the form which said that he agreed with the assessment and would no longer contest or appeal it, and wrote out a check for the full amount. He inked a star by the sentence about not contesting or appealing and wrote in the space provided for "other comments":

I sign this agreement and pay the full amount required but wish to go on record here that I disagree with the auditor's interpretation of my claim. If I had the energy I used to have, I would pursue the matter and believe that I could substantiate my case in tax court. I say this without any feeling of animus toward the auditor, Mr. G. Whipp, whom I found to be a person of humanity.

Wendell W. Spear

[9]

A week later, Frances called him. "Mr. Wool wants to know if you heard from the auditor yet."

"I should have let him know, Frances. I heard a few days ago. There was no change to speak of. I mailed in the check."

"Do you want to speak to him?"

"He's probably composing valentines."

"I think," whispered Frances, "there's a snake in that paradise."

"I won't bother him then, Frances. Tell him that I followed my instinct. And my fatigue."

"Sounds smart to me."

"One of these days, Frances, I'm going to take you to lunch."

"I can't wait, Mr. Spear. I'll tell Mr. Wool. Not about the lunch."

A delightful woman, divorced, if he remembered correctly. Maybe she'd be willing to go to lunch with Mr. Whipp. Who knew what that might lead to. The mysteries of companionship, or, for that matter, of solitude.

[10]

That evening, after his spaghetti and Napa Valley Cabernet, Spear walked the canyon road under the stars. A Pacific wind had blown away the smog; the sky was thick with brightness. Much, he thought now, as it was the night, twenty-six years ago, when he'd heard that Jennifer had been born. At least the audit, thank God, was over.

It was good for you, Spear told himself, as if he were his father in the rectory, backed by walls of literate wisdom, offering his specialty, paternal instruction in asceticism. Everyone needs auditing.

Spear himself had been a strict auditor of those around him. (Except Jennifer.) Amelia had turned from him even before her mother's death. In a way, so had Vanessa. (Dying was her way.) As a critic, too, he'd been famously strict, weighing every film against not only the greatest films but the greatest novels. Some producers had stopped giving him passes.

I was a harsh judge. No wonder they turned away from me. I didn't seek solitude, it was my penalty.

The Ultimate Auditor had put G. Whipp into a terrible body, yet had filled it, filled him, with honey. The mystery of Divine Bookkeeping (whether or not there was a Bookkeeper).

[11]

The next day, Spear fetched the twenty-six volumes of the Loeb Classical Library from his shelves and drove down to the Mobil station. Roger wasn't there, but his grandmother was. "These are Latin books for Roger, Alice. I don't, I can't, read them." He refused the tank of free gas she offered in exchange.

Another oddity: Spear stopped making morning calls to the electronic voices. When he realized that he'd stopped, he erased their numbers from the phone's memory bank and substituted Jennifer's, the Mobil station's, and—surprising himself again, for she had refused to talk to him for years—Amelia's.

★   ★   ★   ★

"Wanna see *Becky's Black Book*? Offers I've had for it you wouldn't believe. Right, it's red, but what it really is is gold. Names here'd knock your eyes out. The deals I could stop. . . .

"Look in the zines, see a guy with girls around, half those girls are mine. [Becky calls to a TV crew from *Hard Copy*: "Like hell I will. You pay for that. I just said no to 20/20."] They'd like me and Tiff roughing. That'd cost 'em. We'll even throw in a stud, though I hate sloppy seconds. [Inspecting herself in ceiling mirror.] Like this wrap-a-round? Norma Kamali. I need a pedicure, but who's got time? . . .

"I'm the center of things here. Not bad for a kid from west of Doheny who didn't get laid till she was eighteen. A redhead animator from Disney. Haven't fucked a redhead since. [Holds up hand and shows a sapphire ring.] Ed Schrosz. Elderly gentleman. He sold me to Madame Rosa for five hundred. I was fucked up on Mandrax. . . . Rosa sent me to these sheiks. Forty thousand which I kept twenty-two of. One time a spender gave me fifty. He said, 'You're nothing but bones.' Imagine if I'd been size 8."

From Becky Faule, in conversation with Rolf Stuppe,
Rebecca of Cunnybrook Farm (Knopf, 1994)

KENERET ⋆ Shooting

[1]

The place: Wilshire, homey old L.A., but shooting toward the black-and-blue glass high-rises, past the bubbling scum of the tar pits, and back to the County Museum's Egyptian facade and into its glass entrails.

The protagonists's situations:

1. Harry Munjak, in the jacket of his camouflage outfit, six weeks back from Vietnam, meets the footloose French beauty Mlle. Laure. It's Harry's crisis time between his return flight to California and his decision to leave job, wife, and children to "do something for myself. I risked myself, discovered myself. I was the puppet of army thugs and a rioting home country. Now Harry is for Harry."

2. Laure DeMeer has come to L.A. from Tahiti where she's been dancing in a nightclub for four years, trying to wash out the disgrace of her father's trial for collaboration with the enemy in WWII. Harry's cousin has picked her up there and offers her a part in a movie he's producing. Now in L.A., the movie's fallen through. She gets a job at the souvenir counter of the L.A. County Museum and begins a love affair with Harry.

Day's action: Harry and Laure rendezvous at the museum, walk across the park to the tar pits. Is she going to go or stay? Is he going to break his life apart?

Resolution: He tells her that she's not the answer to his problems. Stunned, half crazy, she vaults the barrier and throws herself into the boiling scum.

[2]

Keneret had gone down with Leet—she was on payroll now—to scout the museum and park. Grand stuff, the gussied-up tar pits and phony mastodons against the black-and-silver high-rises, plus a few bungalow bits of 1930s L.A. People looked tiny under the steel struts, glass walls, and concrete pillars of the County Museum's Egyptian facade. In its enormous cafeteria, half inside, half on the terrace, they joined the salad-eaters and wine-bibbers, actors, writers, editors, and unit directors between assignments. Keneret ran into Will Buskirk and Mandy Voorst cooking up—what? A play? A fling? They fingerwaved *hi/good-bye*.

Gallery B held the exhibit they were going to use in the film: the "Degenerate Art" Hitler and Goebbels had ripped out of museums and Jewish apartments. He and Leet went through the exhibits, newsreels of the dictator screaming to a screaming audience, soldiers throwing books into a bonfire, hook-nosed Jews glaring at handsome blonds from shopwindows, the posh German crowd at the 1937 exhibition of the paintings and sculptures which surrounded them here and now, sneering at and recoiling from Dix's scarifying portraits, Grosz's red-night *Metropolis*, Kirchner's nightmare self-portrait, Beckmann's *Yellow Christ*.

"What do you think?" Keneret asked her.

"Those times seem long ago as the dinosaurs."

"That's bad," said Keneret. "I don't want our film to smell like a costume picture. This is still alive for me. Maybe because I'm a Jew."

"I didn't know," said Leet.

"You have lived in the sticks, haven't you? I was six when Hitler walked through that Munich exhibition. Of course, I didn't know anything about it till this exhibit, but it's living stuff for me. And should be—because of your father—for you."

"No, because I read and cried about Anne Frank."

"We've got to make them cry too."

They sat on the long terrace with wine and sandwiches, an odd couple on an odd mission. "I'm so far from everything," said Leet. "Fiji. France. My father. I'm not part of anything, except the deli. That you—we—are going to make a movie about something to do with me, that thousands of people who don't know me will know about me—"

"Not thousands. Millions, or we're sunk. And it won't be you up there, it'll be some huge dream of someone a little like you. Nobody understands it. I'm in the business my whole adult life and I don't. I even call it business to help me get away from the illusory part of it. Nothing could be more real than the Nazis, but look at them. Illusionists. They killed for illusions. Got killed for illusions. Maybe that's why they used film so well. Their whole shtick was illusion. Their great leader a hysterical little shoe-clerk type—Chaplin did him perfectly—brave, yes, even foolhardy, an out-of-work veteran, a third-rate artist living on his wits, of which he had a good supply, addled or not. So Goebbels's people filmed this enraged zero in front of ten thousand flaming torches and a hundred thousand *siegheil*ing brownshirts and turned him into the Messiah. Millions, apparently including your papa, saw him in the newsreels and were hypnotized by him. You saw them in the old newsreels there, hysterics cheering the little shithead. The torches, the flags. They still scare me."

"Not me. I think he looks silly. They all do. What was the point of it all? I can't believe my father—an intelligent man, he knew so much, not like me—I don't believe he was fooled by Hitler. He wasn't Nazi. People in Meillac called him the *flamand*, but he loved France."

"And left it."

"Yes. When he thought it hated him."

"Forgive me, Leet," said Keneret, remembering that he was not here to provoke but to get her ready to be Laure. "Your beliefs are important to the film—and to me personally—but our job's to interest people who know next to nothing about that time. A movie doesn't handle complex things very well. It's just a visual story, focused to give lots of very different people clues to make them care for those huge images on the screen. We have to make them fall in love with the characters, the shadows. Or fear them, or hate them. The big thing's not to be bored by them. The audience has to understand, yet be surprised by what they do and say. Half the understanding doesn't come from the story, but because the audience either knows the actors already, stars like Dillon, or knows that attractive new people—like you—are going to be built into stars."

"It won't work with me, Mr. Keneret."

"I think it will. You can do a lot in a dark theater with music and a good story. Even the stuff you find silly will kick in. You'll be surprised how much they'll care for you."

"I will be."

Keneret did not say that he'd be too. "If we can connect Laure's suicide to her father, show how in her mind Harry's desertion of her is a continuation of her father's desertion, we'll have something strong."

"It seems fetched far."

"Far-fetched, yes, but we're going to give them lots of nice things, an interesting story, pretty people, pretty scenery—France, Fiji, Flemishland, all the *F*'s, including the one that almost always works. The story's far-fetched, but Sfaxe has made it logical. Movielogical."

"It's so much stranger than people know."

"Wait'll we start filming. Then you'll see strange stuff. The first sequence we're shooting is down here, at the museum and the tar pits."

"The end of the script."

"Because next week's when we have permission to film here. My job's to know the story so well, the shooting sequence doesn't matter."

[3]

The first few days' rushes were first-rate. They'd done the action scene first, Leet running across the park, up the stone steps of the escarpment. They built the track, rolled the Arriflex 35, wheeled the Apollo crane, bounced the light, marshaled the extras, wrangled the animals—dogs, cats, pigeons—laid out the marks, and let Leet loose. The stunt girl did the jump, then Leet ran to the edge of the bubbling tar and flung out her arms like the Nike of Samothrace.

In motion, she was good. Physical effort put what was needed into her face. Keneret told her, "Remember, he's just abandoned you. You feel you're nothing. Your father's betrayed you, you feel you'll never be anything."

Almost nothing changed in her face, but it didn't matter. Running and leaping supplied enough. When he'd tested her, back in the fall, he'd tried to stir her up. "You're watching a dog being kicked. Your mother's dying . . . you'll never see her again. You've just lost the tournament."

"That's not the way my mind works."

On the set, what absorbed her was the equipment. Between takes, she talked to the grips, the camera crew, the sound mixer. In a week, she was asking about lenses and had figured out, better than he, till he looked through the eyepiece, where the edge of the frame was, where she should stand. She caught on to shadows, highlighting, backlighting; you'd have thought she'd had years in film school. It was only acting that was beyond her, as if the story, her own story, meant nothing to her.

Was the face inexpressive because there was nothing to express? Back in the Wauwausawu Room, when she'd told him her history, her face had been lit with blue and green highlights off the ocean. His desire had seen what he wanted there. He remembered thinking, This is class, not passivity. For film, the right sort of passivity—Keaton's, Cooper's, McQueen's—was beautiful. The camera could make stone look tragic.

When he drove over to Duggan's with her test, he did what Kuleshov had done with students at the Moscow Film Academy, juxtaposed her blank face with totally different events, tragic, comic, neutral. It worked.

"She's very good," said Duggan.

Scholem Vlach, Duggan's dour assistant, saw through it but said nothing. When Duggan asked him what he thought, he said, "We'll all see." Strangely, Duggan, who picked up on everything, let that go by.

[4]

Duggan had loaned five New Objectivity paintings to the "Degenerate Art" exhibit so Keneret was given three days, from 6:00 to 9:00 A.M., to shoot there. (Duggan had also managed to halve the enormous insurance premium.) Keneret shot Leet and Dillon in front of the savage paintings the way Orson Welles had shot Rita Hayworth by the shark tank in *Lady from Shanghai*: the background was the message.

Keneret showed Duggan the rushes in the screening room of his Bel Air château. "First-rate, Ezra," said Duggan. "What you think, Scholem?"

Vlach, one of the six men in Hollywood who still wore neckties, said, "Virtuosity's dangerous." ("The voice of the necktie," Keneret groaned to Marcia.)

Vlach seldom addressed anyone but Duggan, who once explained to an annoyed Keneret, "He's not even speaking to me. I'm only a stand-in for Truth. How a fellow so ill at ease with human beings can know so precisely what they're going to think and feel is—after all my years around him—beyond me."

For twenty years, Duggan had been Keneret's financial ace in the hole. They'd met at the time Duggan was rumored to be buying MGM. Keneret had just made *The Hair of the Dog* there, and Duggan called him in to ask about the studio, the facilities, the personnel, the way it ran. Keneret told him what he knew, and, days later, Duggan withdrew what may or may not have been an offer. Some people blamed Keneret; others thanked him. He knew that the decision had little to do with him, but when he tried to go back to Metro for his next film, he was turned down. Then he was turned down everywhere.

Which is when he heard again from Duggan. "I'd been in his sights all along," Keneret told Spear.

"A glass chip in his mosaic."

"Don't ask me why. For all I know, he's got title to my soul."

"What counts is you can make the picture."

He had made it; a bust.

By now, three Duggan-backed pictures later, Keneret trusted without understanding the financier. Here and there, though never from Duggan, he learned some of his history. Poppa Duggan's family name was something like Stalin's, Djugushvili. Maybe they were cousins. If so, Duggan's PR people had covered it up, along with most of his rear. Where had he grown up? The facts—out of *Current Biography*—were birth and public school in Cleveland, father a shoemaker, mother a housewife. He had a year on scholarship at Western Reserve. No more schooling in sight. The key early fact was the sixteen-year-old Duggan's opening a newsstand with money saved from seven years of odd jobs. At twenty, he owned a dozen newsstands; at twenty-six, he controlled the delivery of newspapers and magazines in much of Cleveland. He bought a racing sheet, a TV guide, a publishing house specializing in health and psychic books, then the first of his seventeen radio and television stations. The buying and selling, merging and dissolving, leveraging and parachuting, went on through the seventies and eighties. The largest augmentation of his billions came from the sale of savings-and-loan companies before they hit the fan.

A compact, dark-faced man with upswept gray hair and a thick mustache, Duggan could have passed for Stalin's brother. Said Marcia, "Nature's way of revealing what Duggan's paid his flacks to conceal. But why doesn't he shave the mustache?"

"Probably enjoys the threat of it," said Keneret. "It's a hell of a mustache."

Duggan was perfunctorily courteous with Marcia, but she felt what almost everyone sensed with him, a high wall of secrecy, perhaps contempt.

Keneret didn't sense it. "I think I reach him. There's just a high price of admission. I pay."

Scholem Vlach was the only male companion Duggan was seen with. (Keneret had seen women in the Bel Air palace.) A Mrs. Duggan was referred to in *Current Biography* as "his high-school sweetheart," and the *L.A. Times* had published a picture labeled MRS. DANIEL DUGGAN but the next day printed a correction, saying there were no available pictures of Mrs. Duggan. No junior Duggans had surfaced, and Duggan's parents were said to be dead.

"Not even Stalin hid things that well," said Marcia. "I don't know how you work with him."

"He leaves me alone, and I know where I stand. I think. It's only the stooge that gives me the creeps. Vlach."

"How?"

"I'm not sure he's the stooge."

[5]

The second week, everything went wrong. It rained four days. They had cover shots, but Keneret, less flexible than he used to be, felt the shooting rhythm altered; worse, his feeling spread to the cast and crew. Zemanski, poking his chest, said, "Something's wrong here, my dear friend. I've got Jew jitters."

"Do your job, Leo. Competent people—Yids too—don't rattle."

Friday, they went out to the dripping pits; the mastodons looked like moth-eaten fur. Lukes used every sort of filter, but nothing could dry out the uneasiness. Dillon Schorr's agent, a foxy malcontent, pulled him off "zis vet set." In the day's rushes, Leet's impassivity showed up as boredom. Saturday, back indoors, Dillon tripped over a lamp cord and bumped a million-dollar Kirchner.

"What the hell's wrong with you?" Keneret screamed, luckily out of the prowling agent's earshot.

"Can't see good. The light's all goofy."

It wasn't the light. Dillon was myopic and vain. At home, he wore eyeglasses; on the set, he'd tried putting in contact lenses and nearly poked his eye out.

"The chump's gotta be able to see," Keneret told the assistant director. "Get soft lenses made, and find someone who can insert them for him."

They shot around him. Monday, an old lady showed up to insert the lenses. She was lame and couldn't drive, so a car and chauffeur had been hired to fetch her from Encino. Dillon's clumsiness and vanity cost them fourteen thousand dollars.

When the rain stopped, and they shot outdoors again, a wind knocked over a scrim which missed Dillon by inches. The stunt girl tripped over it and broke her ankle. Meanwhile Leet kept stumbling over her lines, and her blank face got blanker. It was clear on the rushes, as it was on the set, that she didn't care about the story. Keneret couldn't whip her into motion.

It was one of those dead times which come into filmmaking, but because of the twenty-one-day approval units, it could mean early death. "Why did the bastard put me on trial like this?" Keneret asked Marcia. "After all these years."

Marcia said she thought that it was Vlach figuring that Keneret, cocktrapped by Leet, had cast someone who couldn't, Kuleshoved or not, sustain a movie.

[6]

Friday of the third week they shot near Santa Monica Pier, where Keneret and Leet had talked on her first day in the States after he had her picked up at the airport, driven to the house, introduced her to Marcia, and given her lunch. Back then, they'd walked up Ocean Avenue, past the broken chain of homeless people smoking, eating, drinking, and sleeping at the trestle tables under the palms. Said Keneret, "You know I told you to come only if you'd've come without my being here."

"And sent me the money to come," said Leet. "I couldn't have come without the money."

"The money's one thing. Staying here's another. I've got enough money to give to people I like. I liked you. I like you now. But if you depend on me to stay here, that takes much more than money. Time, thought. Time for you, thought for you. I don't have time; I can't spare thought from my work, my life."

"I thought I was going to be your work."

"So did I, but many things have to happen before that does."

"I don't understand."

"Why not? It's English . . . you understand English."

"I understand English. I don't understand what you mean. You give me money to come, but when I come, you don't want me here. I thought you want to do the movie about my father, to see if I can act in the movie. That's what we talked about. Oh, look, flowers." Wednesday, market day on Arizona Street: a hundred flower, fruit, and vegetable stalls.

"We talked about it, right. But I said I had no idea if it would work. An idea's something that flies through your brain in a second. A movie takes months, maybe years. Hundreds of people, millions of dollars. It's not easy. Getting someone into a movie isn't snapping their photograph. A thousand times out of a thousand and one, nothing comes of it. Nothing."

"I didn't expect—all I expect is to talk with you. To see you and talk."

He looked at her exceptionally clear face. A face in waiting. If a question mark could be a face, it was Leet's face. But even while he hesitated, the face answered itself. "I want to do something, try something. If it doesn't go, I'll try something else. I don't want you to give me money. I want to earn it. Then I'll go—where I go. Back to Naviti. To France, New York.

I don't have time to know anything now. I don't understand anything here. I'm too tired now. Though already, with you, I like it here. I don't understand why."

He bought her a bunch of jonquils.

[7]

Understanding. What did that mean? Linda Sujo, a friend of Marcia's with a Ph.D. in Spending, bought a book on the best-seller list by the physicist Stephen Hawking which Keneret had looked at and put down.

"Can't make anything of it."

Linda said, "I loved it." Since it was a best-seller, thousands of people must be saying that, yet in the *L.A. Times*, a Nobel Prize–winning physicist said he couldn't understand it and said that Hawking himself said that some of the ideas had gotten away from him. But Linda Sujo understood. "Understanding" for her meant brushing up against funny words often enough so that they looked familiar, the way Keneret recognized a couple of the bums on Ocean Avenue. That wasn't knowing them. For Linda Sujo, understanding Hawking was a species of self-gratulatory spending.

Leet's understanding differed from Linda's. She hadn't understood Keneret or he her. She didn't understand the world out of which he came, and he didn't understand that she wouldn't understand that it wasn't a question of her understanding the words, or of her being old enough to know what men said to attractive girls they met in places away from home. She'd traveled thousands of miles, but then, so had geese. She was no goose and had sensed before he had that out there in the middle of the Pacific his appetite had formed his words, and that he'd just seen her in his pan, ready to shove in his oven.

[8]

Three days after Keneret wrote the rough outline, two days after he'd first called Frank Laggio, Marcia went through the West L.A. rental listings with Leet, made calls, drove her around, and approved with her a one-room apartment in a four-story stucco building on Brockton, fifty yards south of Wilshire, a fifteen-minute walk from the deli where, by the time

Laggio was transforming her life into a contemporary love story, she was serving lox and matzo-ball soup to its customers.

More than Keneret's seeing Leet, it was Marcia's helping her which reignited his vision of the lovely girl stranded ten thousand miles from home by her father's old complicity; now, once again, Leet's long legs, short breasts, and clear, interrogative face became the legs, breasts, and face of Laure, the girl of the outline, Laggio's script, and, weeks later, Sfaxe's.

Beginnings are mysterious. Projects, like most children, are conceived in the dark. The core of Keneret's life was the leap from idea to film, a sort of contraplatonism, if he remembered—from Dr. Kuhn's philosophy course at Chapel Hill forty-odd years ago—what that was. Was the beginning here the girl in tennis shorts on the red-clay court, the green mountains behind, the blue sea around her, the beautiful voice sliding over French *u*'s and *r*'s into English syllables? One section of Keneret's head was a book of almost-tactile narratives, some more than fifty years old. Here were the bodies and faces that had excited him, to eighty or ninety of which he'd done what was called making love. Over and over he turned these pages: Jill Winter in fifth grade, leaning over in her peasant blouse so that he saw those strange bumps that he never touched; Kora Craggelet, the cocoa-colored girl he'd persuaded to sneak away from the producer who'd brought her to the Westwood party and with whom he'd spent a terrific hour in the grass behind a greenhouse, smelling her sexual odors overlaid with those of the concealing boxwood; Andrea and Stephanie, the twin whores at the Avignon Festival; starlets, singers, waitresses; the redhead in the RCA Building elevator who put her knees into the backs of his and followed him to an empty office where he told the unknown secretary to take the day off; the mobster's girlfriend; twenty-five or thirty others he could summon up with ease. Many nights, lying beside his beloved wife, the book opened and, stirred by these tactile stories, he made love to them, sometimes with Marcia's help. He'd never told her of his, or asked about her inner book, yet he knew that she *understood* and wouldn't talk or joke about it, knowing his odd verbal prudery.

Leet was now in the book, but instead of the old pursuit—it would surely be useless, at least not worth the trouble—she reenergized the desire to film her.

As for the movie's beginning, it might well be the fifth-grade sight of Jill's breasts or, for that matter, the hatred he felt in Loew's Eighty-third Street movie theater booing the uncomprehended staccato gutturals of Adolf Hitler.

[9]

This monkey business of filmmaking: pictures, chemical emulsions; a hundred, two hundred, five hundred people screwing in bulbs, typing words, mimicking noises (the proud craft of Foley men), driving trucks, painting posters, shipping canisters, writing reviews; selling tickets; and he . . . somehow the center of it. Not its Unmoved Mover, for he was as much moved as mover; more the motion of what would be the motion picture. What was he after? Some heightened yet simplified, at least clarified, depiction of decisive encounters set in artful spaces arranged to speed the pulse of thought, of being, human being, so that the result would be and perhaps stay part of every viewer's own interior book, a guide to and transfiguration of existence. And this for a few dollars, and without—at least physical—risk.

Important work? As important as many things. And work that required more labor, thought, and skill than most. It was what he did, what most of his life was for.

So when things began going wrong with the film, Keneret, more experienced, even readier for failure, than he'd been twenty and thirty years ago, was now less able to endure it.

[10]

The worst downer happened at the end of the third week: they lost Lukes. (And, as a sort of punctuation in gloom, the very next day, there was bad news about Simeon Slobos.)

It was the day a suburban jury exonerated policemen who'd beaten a black motorist to a pulp yards away from a fourteen-year-old videotaper's window. Within minutes of the broadcast announcing the verdict, South-Central L.A. burst apart, and within minutes of that, Floyd Harmel was on the phone to Keneret begging for half a day of Lukes's time. "No other cameraman in reach can shoot so fast and well. I'm begging you, Ez. There's no time to waste. All I need's three hours, four. It can't be duplicated," followed by a spate of promises and bribes (a quarter point of the movie).

"Okay," said Keneret, if Lukes was willing. He was, and ten minutes later, Harmel's van swung by.

That night, Harmel, dead voiced, called again. "We cruised up and down East L.A., Brighton, Normandie, Halldale. Jimmy Bludsoe, a black guy from the neighborhood, drove. We're behind one-way glass; no way you could see the camera. It was something. Sheer craziness. Scary and beautiful. First time since the war I'd filmed real-life action. Totally different. I'm pointing here, there, Luke's pointing, filming, Jimmy's driving like crazy. We're out of our minds keeping cool. I had no idea—maybe I'd just forgotten that people in the grip of feeling fall into classic poses. You see them actually turn into art. A woman holds a man hit by a rock in her arms: Pietà. A Korean grocer protecting his shop, holds his arms out like a Crucifixion. Molotov-cocktail throwers are Davids. People, animals, objects are wild and mad as *Guernica*. Lukes said, 'I don't know if I'm shooting a tornado or the Uffizi.'

"And *boom*, a Molotov cocktail, on the hood. I'm on the floor, blood's storming over my head, I can't see. When I can, it's Lukes bleeding over me. I yell, 'Jimmy, get us outta here. A hospital.' We drive like crazy, we're rattling around, Jimmy's yelling, 'We've had it, we're trapped.' I've got Lukes's head wrapped in my shirt, he's going fast, I know it. Ten minutes more, he wouldn't have made it."

"He's alive?"

"Yes. He's okay."

"He's okay?"

"He's going to be okay. I'm sure."

Okay, alive, but out of action.

So they had no cinematographer.

That night, Guy Chen called Keneret and asked if the crew should come in.

"Absolutely," said Keneret. "It's a setback, but I'll have someone to-morrow or the next day. We can do second-unit stuff for a day or two. Stick with me, Guy. Don't worry about a thing."

But worry was what there was.

The next day, over breakfast, Marcia, white with surprise, read aloud an item from the *Times:* Si Slobos and his accountant, Zachary Wool, had been indicted for tax evasion.

"Not possible," said Keneret. "Si, maybe; not Zack. He won't let clients fudge a nickle. He's pure honor."

"Wendell said he'd gone loopy over some woman."

"Too strong. He's male. Period. He bought a Lexus. So what? The IRS probably has something on Slobos. Maybe. His deals are so complex who can say. This way, they scare everybody. That's why they pull in Zack. They hope he'll scare enough to come up with what they don't have. I don't like it, but I know it'll be all right."

"It won't affect the picture—or you?"

Keneret rubbed his face, thinking. "Does one ever know the effect of anything? Sure, money people know Si has a piece of the film, and some'll get nervous. The nervous are always nervous. Wool's something else. The IRS could go through his clients' returns. But I don't think they'll find anything in our stuff. Or Wendell's." More rubbing. "Am I sure? Hell no. 'Sure' has been a dirty word since ape-men saw their shadows."

But in the next hour, he had calls from Stan Oxenhandler and Leo Zemanski asking where they stood. "Same place as yesterday," said Keneret. "We're on course. Half speed for a day or two. I've got calls in to the ASC; we'll have someone in for Lukes in two days. As for Slobos, I could cover his piece myself. No worry. I show the rushes to Duggan on Saturday."

To Zemanski, he added, "You think Ella might want to take Slobos's little piece of the pie, Leo?"

"I'll ask, my dear friend, but when it comes to my spouse's purse, it's tight as a sheeny's ass."

Keneret managed not to explode—as Zemanski clearly wanted him to. Not today, anyway.

[11]

Saturday night, after the rushes were screened in Duggan's screening room, Duggan, Vlach, and Keneret sat in the dark for a long ten seconds. Even before Vlach touched up the lights, Keneret understood.

"Let's talk in the library," said Duggan. He led; Keneret followed; Vlach buttoned the rear. They walked through a gold corridor hung with Sisleys, Pissaros, and Corots, frames capped with proprietary lights under metal brows, through a sitting room, a music room, a terrace centered by a fountain sculpted with fish and cherubs. Keneret paused for a second's breath of boxwood-scented air and was run into by Vlach, who grunted not *Excuse me* but "Christ." Ten yards ahead, Duggan held the door, not looking back. A reproach. A plum-colored hall lit with the lights over two Kandinskys, then the library, an intimidation of gold-tooled leather sets, folios, quartos, and octavos bound in dolphin-stamped morocco, a few million dollars of the world's wisdom there to ratify their possessor and condemn his inferiors. Three armchairs, scarlet and green satin, in a triangle around a seventeenth-century Spanish traveling desk converted into a table. Light sprayed from sources hidden in the shelves and frescoed ceiling. (The frescoes were Tiepolo clouds and seraphim.) The light was sufficient to make out faces, not to study them. A bottle of Dom Pérignon was canted in a bucket of dry ice; three gold-figured goblets stood on Damascus coasters. Whatever happened here was to be sealed by magnificence. Thought Keneret, A setup, but a small bird of hope still chirped away in him.

At some signal from Duggan—hand, eye, mustache, Keneret didn't see it—Vlach noiselessly popped the champagne and filled the glasses.

Duggan took his up in both hands, drew inspiration from the bubbles, and said, "To you, Ezra. And the good years we've had." He levered his forearm and held, inclining the goblet to Vlach's. They did not let these thousand-dollar goblets touch one another.

Keneret did not raise his, an act of will; the toast was not one he wanted, but the other two goblets waited for his in the air, a gesture was not yet called for; his joined theirs. No lover of champagne, he found it wonderful now.

Said Duggan, "You saw what Scholem and I saw. All week we've seen it coming."

"It's been a hard week."

"Yes. Very bad. Very unlucky."

"But I've never known a production without weeks like it."

"'It'?"

"Hard times. Poets alone at their desk have them. So eighty people, outdoors—"

"Lucky fellows, poets," said Duggan. "Work alone."

"Wish I could. I'm in the wrong business. But I will never again let an agent on the set. Never lend out my cameraman."

"We depend on agents," said Duggan.

"Not on the set."

"Von Stroheim's dead, Ezra," said Vlach.

"I'm not his vintage. I came out after the second war."

"Scholem meant the conditions that used to obtain out here no longer do."

"You're informing a man who's been out here forty years and has spent the last weeks nursing Dillon Schorr. And extracting pathos from stone." What an odd face this shithead Scholem has, thought Keneret, sighting it over his golden goblet. Almost triangular, like an arrowhead. With him as its target. He'd known it, maybe from the beginning, and surely all week, surely when he drove up to Bel Air with his spools of film, known it against the odds that he was wrong, the hope that Duggan would understand. Understand what? Understand him. Stand under him. Back him. Trust him. He was still who he was. Better, he knew more, felt more, remembered more. Which meant he could put more into the films. Given a chance. A real chance, not a twenty-one-day unit chance.

"Scholem was telling me about this book on Einstein he's reading. Very great personality."

"Yes," said Keneret, taking the left turn. "I thought for years there'd be a film in him." What the hell. He'd only put a few months into this. What was that? What were three weeks of rushes? Einstein was a great subject, covered many of the same years. They could even use the "Degenerate Art" exhibit footage.

"Scholem says he had twenty of the greatest productive years any— what do you call them?—physicist ever had."

"Nineteen-three to twenty-three," said Vlach.

"Then? Though he was always brilliant and wonderful, a wonderful man—didn't hurt that he looked like God—he got off the train, wasn't in touch, spent twenty years working on what didn't count."

"Same with Newton," said Vlach.

"Newton, hm. You didn't tell me that, Scholem. More champagne."

Vlach poured and said, "Shakespeare quit in his forties, went back to his hometown, bought a big house. Occasionally they brought him in to fix up someone else's script, but he knew when to retire."

"I'm not finished," said Keneret.

"Scholem and I think you are, Ezra."

★   ★   ★   ★

"Laemmle wanted a share of this vamp pie, so that's how I came to this Cloud-Cuckoo-Land. I'd done *Mist* and was filming *Raven Lover* in Budapest when I got the offer. (*Summons* is more like it.) I didn't want to leave Europe, but Papa had lost his job, there was no money for films, and you, *chèrie*, were in my belly. So we boarded the *Bremen* with everything we owned. A month later, we were staring at orange trees from a stucco château with six chimneys, a swimming pool, and more plumbing than in all Budapest. Your *maman* went to work, and didn't need a Sternberg to tell her how to kiss and piss. I talked to cameramen, electricians, assistant directors, I'd already read *Film als Kunst*, I'd been in the theater, I'd done four films, I knew the difference between film action and stage. I could move slowly, legs, arms, eyebrows. I knew where the arc light should go to catch the tips of my hair. I could sniff a burnt-out bulb thirty yards away. There was no problem with voice, even my accent. You know my ear is perfect. I picked up American like a shot. I was musical—nine years of pianoforte—I could move—five years of ballet. Above all, I didn't care if it stopped. When Thalberg borrowed me for *Czarina*, I knew what I was worth, and if they didn't, too bad. I had you, and, for a while, Papa. What else did I need? *Rien du tout.*

"You loved the studio. By the time you were eight, you knew more about makeup and costume, shadows and silence, than most directors. I kept you from those spoiled Hollywood children; you had only the best, swimming pool, dogs, bodyguards—after the Lindbergh baby—and discipline. You spoke three languages, you learned history with researchers and costume people.

"How could I not be proud of you, my beautiful *chèrie?* My own Regina."

"But Maman. At fifteen I was a drunk. I was miserable, terrified, knew nothing and no one. I wanted to die. Every single morning, I didn't want to wake up. "

From Regina Delliger, *Chère Maman: A Celluloid Life*
(Harcourt Brace Jovanovich, 1984)

SPEAR ★ Grandpa

[1]

For Christmas, Jennifer Abarbanel went AWOL. That is, she didn't spend it in St. Louis with her parents but with her grandfather in San Francisco. Here, as an associate of Schmidt, Barczyk & Cole, she worked in her own electronically packed cubicle on the twenty-fourth floor of number 2 Embarcadero Center. On the phone to Spear, she said, "I want to show you what you paid for, Grandpa."

"Helped, Fer. Slightly. But I do want to see it. At least you in it."

In many ways, Spear felt closer to Fer than to anyone he'd ever known. The feeling had intensified over the years, but it began the day Amelia told him that she was pregnant. The night his son-in-law phoned with the news—"Jennifer's arrived, Grandpa, all seven pounds, six ounces of her"— Spear walked the canyon road outside his old Beverly Glen house in a strange state. He'd been a father twenty-eight years, but—as he thought about it that night—fatherhood had been zoological and egocentric rather than thoughtful and social, a sort of chest-pounding semiaggression which certified manliness: *See what I did*. Grandfatherhood was mental, almost abstract. There was a dignity in it which completed him in a way father-hood hadn't. It meant that, somehow or other, he'd done his duty, raised or helped raise someone well enough so that she'd wanted—and had—her own child. It made him a richer part of the social order, the founder of a dynasty, not just the lusting, accidental discharger of seed. Or so he'd thought that night, walking among cypress and palms under the stars, imagining the seven-pound, six-ounce person whom he'd never seen, heard, or touched, but who was, somehow, his.

A few weeks before Christmas, Spear had read an Updike story which ended with the protagonist holding his just-born granddaughter and thinking, "No one belongs to anybody, except in memory." Spear thought Updike a wonderful, if chilly, writer, but this didn't strike home. Sure, it was only in memory, at least in the mind, that relationships and feelings existed; language transmitted what the body couldn't. Yet if the grammatical possessives *mine* and *my* were mental, they stood for something real. Jennifer wasn't chattel, but she was his, his grandchild, not Updike's, not anyone else's (except her other living grandpa, Grandpa Abarbanel, and two dead grandmothers). It was not *owning* so much as *belonging*. He and Jennifer, for better or worse, belonged to each other. (*Belonging*, cousin of *longing, needing, wanting, enjoying*, even—to use the frayed participle Spear seldom used—*loving*.)

Jennifer's arrived, Grandpa. All seven pounds, six ounces, of her.

Spear had opened a bottle of Mumm's and toasted Vanessa: "Here's to you, Grandmother." A rare smogless night, and the stars, those flaming hints of far more terrifying immensities, looked like signs of a benign, perhaps even benevolent, design of which, in some incomprehensibly significant way, he, Wendell Wallace Spear, son of Angelica and Malcolm, father of Amelia, and now grandfather of Jennifer Abarbanel, was an infinitesimal part, a part which belonged to every other part. The petite new layer of generation had somehow rounded the Spear component of creation, made its plane geometry solid, formed a cosmos out of almost-haphazard chaos.

Walking the bright road, a white band under a white moon, Spear felt an intimacy, even a friendliness, in infinite space. One day—who knows—Jennifer Spear Abarbanel Something-or-Other—if girls still took their husband's name, if there were still such things as husbands—might be walking this very road, celebrating the birth of her granddaughter, his great-great one. (Of course Jennifer would inherit the house, inherit everything he had, photographs, letters, CDs, videos, what was left of his film library. She already had his genes.) And maybe her granddaughter would walk here as well—if human beings still walked, if there were still roads to walk on, if California, if the earth, still existed.

The next day he phoned Keneret. "I had no idea it would be so different from paternity. Why hasn't it been written about more? You know that Ghirlandaio painting of an old fellow with a wart looking at his beautiful grandson? I don't think there's a literary equivalent. Maybe the grandmother in Proust, but she's seen through the boy's eyes, so it's more feeling than thought."

"I suppose most people before—when? the nineteenth century?—didn't know their grandpas. There is that great scene in *Godfather I*, Corleone scaring his grandson with the orange peel in his mouth, just before he keels over."

"Film doesn't explain."

"And Ghirlandaio?"

"A Mafia family's different: it's against the world. This way, you join the world. You're an old single-gauge track merging with the system."

"You are high, Wendell."

"I am, and I haven't even seen the little thing. Yet I love her; whatever that promiscuous verb means. I love the idea of her, but also love her. She's mine. My granddaughter."

"I should envy you, but, for some reason, that sort of thing means nothing to me."

"Why should it? It's unearned, undeserved. Unless you get points for raising a child who wants a child of her own."

"I don't think Grandpa and Grandma Hitler should get points."

[2]

As long as they could remember, Spear and Jennifer had been friends, allies, and partners as well as what they were—grandfather and granddaughter. He couldn't remember a single word they'd exchanged that wasn't inflected by admiration, joshing, concern, affection.

Perhaps distance had intensified their relationship. Jennifer had lived two thousand miles away in St. Louis until she went off to school in Northampton, Mass., a thousand miles farther away. He usually saw her only twice a year, Christmas and summer. Her junior year abroad, he didn't see her at all, and then Amelia had shut him out for another year. (He'd decided not to go behind her back to see Jennifer.) After her graduation four years ago, she'd come to California for law school and then begun her legal career in San Francisco with Schmidt, Barczyk & Cole, twelve hundred miles closer to him.

She'd taken and passed the bar exam that first September—"the worst days of my life, Grandpa, I was too nervous to pee"—and he hadn't seen her. When she agreed that they spend Christmas together, she said she only had three days off and that he'd be alone the rest of the week.

"I'm good at being alone. You'll be more—at least better—society than I've had in years."

[3]

To fill out his time, and to make Christmas even more a family affair, Spear called his only American cousin, Hugh Wallace, and suggested that they rendezvous in San Francisco. Hugh's son, Timothy, lived down the peninsula in Santa Clara County. A couple of years ago, when Jennifer was in law school at Davis and Tim was forming a band in Santa Cruz, the old cousins introduced the young ones to each other. They might be friends and perhaps something more. Fer was twenty-five, Timmy three years older.

Twenty-five seemed old as well as young to Spear, who thought decades back to when he was teaching English in Versailles and living in a French *pension*. Every morning, the squirrel-faced maid, Lucille, stooped under the attic beam to bring him his morning roll and coffee. One day, Spear, feeling the heat from her blouse—or was it the coffee?— asked how old she was. "*Moi*," she said, "*je danse la Catherinette*," and, seeing his puzzlement, said, "It means I'm twenty-five and have no husband." Spear, himself twenty-one, lost his desire but not his feeling for her. "Some lucky man will marry you before long, Lucille." The week before, he'd met Vanessa Legriet at a Paris film club; eleven months later, they were the parents of Jennifer's mother; and, a month after that, married in the Versailles *mairie*.

For decades, he'd made a virtue of this youthful marriage and paternity. He told his father, "It'll s-s-s-stop my catting around, make me b-b-buckle down to work."

"Nothing but exhaustion or castration stops what you call catting around. Not whiskey, not age, and certainly not—with apologies to your good mother—marriage."

Timidity and its consequence, abstinence, had, many years now, stopped it for Spear, but the thought of its stopping—or never beginning, what did he know?—for his wonderful granddaughter dismayed him. He'd read enough journalistic demography to know her generation's Malthusian need to diminish the human swarm. Would she end up as forlorn as chinless Lucille?

Cousin Hugh had married and fathered late, and Timmy was Jennifer's contemporary. They'd make—the cousins told each other—a grand match, though Timmy did not seem much of a marrier. He'd dropped out of UCal Santa Cruz in his freshman year and made an unsure living playing guitar in bands. In the past four years, he'd earned just enough to live without paternal handouts. Spear liked him. He was sensible, curious, amusing, decent, maybe a bit innocent, but Spear liked innocence, especially connected to Fer. A Jennifer-Timmy match ran toward genetic peril, but Spear's grandparents had been first cousins, three of their children lived into their nineties, and there were no—recorded—monsters. Tim would be good to Fer, he'd amuse her, ease the tension of legal ferocity; she would steady him, make him sensible and businesslike. She'd also bring in a good income: even now, as an associate, she made eighty-five thousand a year.

[4]

His first two days in San Francisco, Spear had time to himself. Fer worked till six or seven, and Hugh wasn't flying in till Christmas afternoon. Timmy had a Christmas gig in Sacramento and wasn't arriving till the twenty-sixth. Fine.

Spear liked San Francisco. Once he got used to climbing the streets, he liked walking past the lollipop-colored houses so amazingly canted on the hills; he liked the kitsch exoticism of the Asian neighborhoods, the temples, restaurants, groceries, and knickknack shops. Twenty years alone in the Malibu hills, he hardly realized how much time went by without his seeing or even speaking to anybody on the phone. San Francisco was a party.

Fer had given him an early Christmas present, a ticket to the Exploratorium, the science museum. "There's an exhibit you'll like, Grandpa. People tape for three or four minutes what they think about love. You can play their tapes, and you can make one yourself."

"I'm no specialist in that department."

"If you know one, I should consult her."

Fer had very fair skin, a terrific giveaway for feelings. Her blush here pained Spear. He never wanted to discomfort let alone hurt her. What did she have to keep from him? They weren't—were they?—like so many grandfathers and granddaughters, stock figures who spoofed or gushed over each other. They were friends, people who relied on each other, and not just in emergencies. Yet he'd seen so little of her. He wasn't busy, but she was: college, law school, work. A monthly phone call and a semiannual visit left all the room in the world for ignorance of each other. "You're more lovable. . . . I'd love to hear anything you'd say."

"When I know something about it, maybe I'll make one."

"You know much more—y-y-you wouldn't be w-w-what you are, if you didn't. And you'll know a lot more d-d-damn soon. Or American men are even d-d-d-dumber than I think they are."

"At least I know I love you."

"Well, yes, and I you. Of course. But you'll see, if you haven't yet, there's something very different out there."

[5]

The 22 bus stopped across Columbus Avenue from his motel. (Fer had offered him her bed—"I'll take the couch"—but Spear needed space and solitude. Even in St. Louis, where his daughter had a large house, he'd usually stayed in motels. Was that something else that had irked her?) Eleven o'clock, he had the bus almost to himself. It set him to thinking, first about the tape. What three minutes could he leave behind for visitors, research psychologists, for Fer and Fer's children? In his cabin, he spent many hours looking at pictures and old cardboard-backed daguerreotypes of his parents, grandparents, and great-grandparents. In them, somewhere, clues were transmitted. Yet they were silent; the tape would speak.

Love.

The abused and overused word contained—and concealed—much. Updike and Roth, two of Spear's erotic authorities, didn't deal with love at all. If anything, their characters' sexual sagas excluded love. Lovers were each other's motif, outlet, occasion of relief and exaltation, almost second selves, not just theaters of each other's seductive and sexual performances. As for the last, Spear, their reader, realized how limited his own virtuosity had been even when lust and passion dominated every day and night. He'd been a banal lover. His feelings, though, had not been banal, or, if banal, still enormous; but he'd never worked up a vocabulary for them. Only occasionally, writing about a movie, did he try to analyze the singular, immense, and—as far as he could learn—invented elements of love. To compare the feelings of Rhett and Scarlett, Bogart and Bergman, with Dante's feelings for Beatrice or Pierre Bezukhov's for Natasha—even when reviewing movie versions of *War and Peace*— hadn't been in his critical compass. As for his own feelings, he'd let them remain inarticulate, protected first by his stutter, then, in France and America, by his English accent. Whatever he'd uttered in the way of courtship or lyric articulation was too embarrassingly banal to remember.

The bus was passing a huge sand-colored school outside which Spear saw two young girls, eleven or twelve, chattering, gesturing. One, strawberry haired, leaned against a lamppost, left foot, toes down, behind the right one in some ballet position. The spontaneous beauty of this Degas-like form almost took his breath away. Did her grandfather realize what a treasure he had?

Which somehow led Spear to think of Jennifer's other grandfather, Felix Abarbanel, a man he'd talked to only a dozen times, but for whom, even now, as the bus turned off Bay onto Cervantes, he felt much affec-

tion. A charming, rosy-cheeked man of the world, Abarbanel was the closest Spear had come in his own person to *entre-deux guerres* European culture. Abarbanel's émigré story was far richer than Spear's. A musician,
born in Istanbul of Sephardic, Spanish-speaking parents, Abarbanel had
studied composition in Lausanne with Kurt Weill, been a choral and
opera conductor in Aachen, Strelitz, Vienna, and Paris, then Bruno Walter's assistant in Berlin. In December 1932, Walter had tipped him off to
what was coming: he'd just heard "Vive Hitler!" shouted at him from the
balcony of Salle Pleyel. "This is a Jewish earthquake, Felix." Three weeks
later Walter had left for London, and a week after that, Abarbanel was
off, bag, baggage, and baton, for Istanbul, then, after six blank months,
Melbourne, where he conducted opera. "Wagner one night, Verdi the
next. English singers," he told Spear. "All discipline and modesty. No
temperament. Five perfect years. Then I did something stu-pid. Eddie
Johnson invited me to the Met. My big chance. Some chance! A zoo of
prima donnas and tenors. No ensemble, no modesty, no discipline, only
megalomaniac soloists counting curtain calls. Two years in that pit, and
then, *Dios gracias*, St. Louis called me. First assistant, then *chef
d'orchestre*. I taught the chorus, the singers, conductors too, nice American men and women. Modesty, discipline, ensemble. The heartland.
That's what it was for me. Ab-so-lute-ly."

Out of Grandpa Abarbanel came stories—some of them pointless; it
didn't matter to entranced Spear—about the artists who created and stood
for what they both loved. The names alone were beautiful to him: Weill,
Hindemith, Stravinsky, Bartók, Toscanini, Walter, Flagstad, Melchior,
Balanchine, Markova, Ashton (the last two as English as Spear himself),
Picasso, Brecht, Braque, Gide, the Mann brothers, and the moviemakers,
Lang, Pabst, Murnau, Lubitsch, von Sternberg. Abarbanel had known
most of them, the artists who'd given the timid, stuttering, bird-watching,
English public-school boy Wendell Spear his idea of what was admired
but never supplied in his father's Devonshire rectory or in the second-
rate public school on the edge of the moors where he'd lived for four
years before Cambridge. In his third year at Cambridge, Spear heard Sieg-
fried Kracauer lecture about the German films of the twenties—*Caligari*
led straight to Hitler—and discovered his vocation. After a year teaching
English in a French lycée, he immigrated to California.

In the early 1950s, Hollywood was thick with European refugees. (Abarbanel himself had spent ten months there conducting film scores for Max Steiner.) They were patronized, indulged, then either ignored or used by the older immigrants, the founders and bosses of the studios. About these tyrants, the young English critic, Wendell Spear, wrote in an essay for *Film Quarterly*:

> *Molochs of anticreativity; flesh merchandising quasi pedophiles full of sanctimonious mendacity. They exhibit the pompous viciousness of Mussolini, if not the lethal Wagnerian hatreds of Herr Schickelgruber-Hitler.*

In time, Spear's prose quieted down and migrated from *Film Quarterly* to *The Nation* and the *Hudson Review*, then, for five years, to the *Los Angeles Times*. Edgy essays had given way to relaxed, though never benign, critical and historical overviews of the film world. Respected and respectable, Spear became a judge on award committees, a semipopular writer and lecturer. (Oddly, within weeks of his arriving in California, his stutter had more or less disappeared.) Then he'd stopped writing and lecturing regularly, bought a five-room cabin in a Malibu canyon, and moved there. In time, Vanessa dead, Amelia grown and flown, he'd turned slowly into what Keneret, his only close friend, called "a semicivilized semihermit."

[6]

The love tape section of the Exploratorium was at the back of the enormous geodesic dome. No one seemed to be around. Spear called into the darkness which surrounded the lit counter, "Anybody here?" A door opened and out came a young man, perhaps Korean, face studded with acne.

"Youwannamakatape?" he said politely.

"I think so, please."

"In here." A light switched on and Spear was pointed to a glassed-in room furnished with a kitchen chair and table in front of a mounted camera. Behind the chair was a screen. "What background?"

"Excuse me?"

"Sea? Mountain? Meadow? Cows?"

"Sea, I think." Spear sat and was handed a card which explained that he was being instructed by an Explainer.

"Whakindamusic?"

"Excuse me?"

"Choose a musical background, R-and-B, country, rock, baroque . . ."

"Baroque sounds right for me."

"Brandenburg Concerto Number Two okay?"

"Why not."

The young man clipped a thumbnail-sized microphone to the lapel of Spear's blazer. "When I leave the room, a red light goes on." He looked expectantly at Spear, who nodded his comprehension and faced the glass nozzle. Above the camera, a red light blinked and the Brandenburg Concerto filled the room. Behind the glass, the Explainer held up a sign: T-A-L-K.

"L-l-love," said Spear. "W-w-what do I m-mean by 'l-love'?"

[7]

He and Jennifer were invited to the family Christmas Eve party of Shari Morgan, another associate at Schmidt, Barczyk & Cole.

"Awfully nice of them to take us in," said Spear.

"Shari says they're thrilled to meet my celebrity grandpa."

"If I'm their idea of celebrity, they must be out of it."

"Shari's dad's read your books."

"Bizarre." But Spear was pleased and bought two bottles of good champagne for the party.

He was always surprised at how small San Francisco was, how quickly, compared with Los Angeles, one arrived where one was going. At the same time, it was intricately divided, and when Jennifer and her friends discussed going to this restaurant or that, they made it sound as complex as New York.

The Morgans lived in Presidio Heights on another hill of three-story gingerbread houses, which, because of the tilt and moonlit shadows, looked to Spear like a set from *Caligari*.

Within minutes, the Morgans, their cousins, and friends made Spear feel that he and Jennifer were a necessary part of their Christmas, a part they never again wanted to do without. His admirer, Howard, owner of a Chevrolet dealership in San Mateo—"Made more money than I ever dreamed or wanted"—had not only read his books but quoted a sentence from one of them about Joan Crawford's acting: "A form of exorcism that wants to get rid of everything but her makeup." When Spear flinched, Howard asked if he'd misquoted it.

"Unfortunately not."

"Then you called her 'an erotic slime pit.' You must have done her in."

"Nature did. I only posted the sign."

They sat in black leather chairs by a fire which shot gold bits around the room into bowls filled with gluhwein and silver platters of petits four. Spear sank into a humane hospitable noise unlike any he'd known in all his Los Angeles decades. He'd never been with such a congregation of more or less ordinary people, lawyers, doctors, merchants, executives, teachers, and patrons of bookstores, galleries, concerts, plays. What a fine cornucopia, he thought. Where have I been?

Shari, a pop-eyed, somewhat manic girl, kept bringing people, one after another, to his armchair.

"Am I the Queen Mother?"

"King for a day," she said, then hustled Jennifer off to meet her older brother, Colin, here from Pittsburgh for the Christmas party. Spear saw them settle into a dark corner. He made out Jennifer throwing her head back and laughing, then later, shaking her forefinger at the man's head.

Over the years, Spear had met a few of Jennifer's friends, but—he realized now—he'd never seen her alone with a man and knew next to nothing about the romantic, the sexual, part of her life. For all he knew, she was gay, though he'd stifled this thought. Why go against the grain of probability till it was necessary? (Ockham's Razor was the one that shaved his thoughts.) It comforted him seeing her easy way with Colin Morgan, who, God knows, might—Spear leapt in an un-Ockhamian direction— pin his name on the next generation of Spears.

A phrase came to him—Hegel's, he thought—"Walking around in marital shoes." It had to do with the mixture of lust and nest-hunger that Spear remembered feeling during his own courtship of Vanessa Legriet. Jennifer, maybe Jennifer's generation, though he disliked such un-

Ockhamian expansions, seemed pinched by such shoes. Perhaps this was why he was wearing them for her.

During dinner, she and Colin sat side by side. Spear watched her touch her head to his shoulder, his hand stroke her hair. The velocity of everything, he thought. An hour ago, they'd never seen each other.

[8]

Christmas morning, he climbed—as he felt it in his leg muscles and chest—Filbert Street for bacon and eggs in front of the little pine Jennifer had decorated the day before he came.

She'd already telephoned her parents in St. Louis to say she was expecting him. Her mother said nothing about it.

"Mom's so strange about you," she said to Spear.

"She got strange. I don't know when or want to know why."

"She keeps more and more of herself to herself. Maybe there's less and less self."

"She was exceptionally open as a little girl. Open and happy. I'm not the only one who thought so."

"I have no idea if she's happy or unhappy."

"She's probably unhappy that you're with me. That chip doesn't get smaller."

"What put it there, Grandpa?"

"She thinks I did, I think. If I plead ignorance, she thinks that's my cover to keep doing the bad things I do. What they are, she doesn't tell me."

"Or me. 'I'll tell you someday' is her line. Wouldn't work in a witness box."

"Our moving to the canyon disturbed her. I'd taken her mother away from her life so I could enjoy mine. Then your grandmother died. There are probably ten other things. She might not know what they are."

"Or won't face."

"Maybe it's genetic. My father was an unhappy man."

"Mom is a hidden—here's another stock word—depressive. And—another—paranoid. A blamer. Though I only heard her blame you once."

"Yes?"

"She said you tried to buy my affection."

"That's an indictment of grandfathers in general." Groaning. "Poor girl." He leaned over and kissed his unhappy daughter's daughter. "Enough. This is too good a Christmas to spoil. I had enough spoiled Christmases."

"In St. Louis?"

"Never there. In England. Your poor great-grandpa hated writing sermons. He despised every word he wrote and thought everyone else did. Christmas the church was full, even atheists showed up to ridicule what he already knew was ridiculous. I never saw anyone so riddled with self-doubt and fear of ridicule, of criticism. His unhappiness filled the house. Thank God you didn't inherit that gene."

"Didn't I?"

Spear didn't want to hear that; he held up his hand and shook his head.

[9]

Jennifer's present to him was an alpaca sweater, which he put on. "Am I a dreamboat?"

"You know you are. I'll have to carry a shotgun."

"How did you find the time to make it?"

"I hardly had time to buy it."

His presents for her were three new novels and four CDs (Mozart chamber music and Barber's *Knoxville: Summer 1915*).

"Too much, Grandpa. You bought the affection long ago." She pulled him to his feet. "Eleven. We better fetch Hugh."

[10]

Driving the Bayshore Freeway, Spear asked her what she thought of Colin Morgan.

"I liked him. Wish I didn't."

"Why?"

"He comes out here only once or twice a year."

"And . . . ?"

"That's my pattern."

"What?"

"Liking people who're difficult—or impossible. I don't know what Shari thought she was doing. Maybe she wants Colin to have a girl in every port."

"My guess is she wants the best for him."

"Oh, Grandpa. Such rosy glasses."

[11]

One day, Spear knew, age would break his cousin, but, at seventy-five, Hugh seemed the Hugh he'd always known. His white hair had enough old strands to enable Spear to see him as a redhead. The blue eyes were clear, his laugh one that made everyone who heard it laugh. The son of Spear's mother's sister who'd married an American soldier in 1918 and joined him in Kansas City a year later, Hugh had gone to the University of Kansas in Lawrence and graduated into World War II. He'd fought in North Africa, Sicily, and Italy. For him, the campaigns were remembered as larks, full of girls, gambling, and farcical stories of military craziness, death, and near death. Demobilized, he failed in five businesses and three marriages. Still, in the thousand hours Spear had spent with him, Hugh was never down, always ready for cards, horses, roulette, women, travel (taking off on the spur of a whim for Vegas, Paris, Nairobi). Everywhere, there were Hugh friends, their houses, boats, and money his to use. As his was theirs. At sixty, he found his métier, importing and selling fine watches, which in the Hollywood of the mideighties became the conspicuously inconspicuous signs of power-wealth. Hundred-thousand-dollar Patek Philippe Calibres, Chopard Imperiales, Rolex Oysters, and Vacheron Constantins gleamed in the wrist hair of L.A. centi-million-aires. Three years ago, Hugh sold the business for six million dollars and now spent his life sailing, playing squash, gambling, investing, learning French—"for the songs of Jacques Brel"—and taking forty-, fifty-, and sixty-year-old women to spas, casinos, and bed. The only things he missed—he told his cousin—were the sexual vigor of his fifties and a grandchild.

Now, in his thousand-dollar plaid sport coat, Hugh embraced Jennifer and Spear, then a woman who'd been his seatmate on the plane. "No, never saw her before. She's on the verge of leaving her husband, found him in their barn, ramming some prospective lamb chops, one of each sex."

"Not sheepish herself," said Spear.

"Right, though she said that next time we'd really have to let our hair down."

"Too bad you had a short flight."

"Everybody traveling wants to tell you his life story. Motion's like whiskey."

"You're what Santa should bring everybody," said Jennifer. "You and Grandpa spoil me for other men."

[12]

The next night, the two old cousins followed the two young ones, Jennifer and Timmy, first ten, then twenty, finally fifty yards back, the young ones holding up while the elders huffed and puffed up and down Chestnut and Polk, Lombard and Larkin, till they gathered at the restaurant where the old ones tucked away half again as much risotto and Chianti as the younger.

"San Francisco makes me ravenous," said Hugh, spooning in the abandoned half of his son's tiramisu.

Ten years older than Spear, muffin shaped, a cigar smoker and drinker, Hugh was hardly bothered by the hills. Of course, Spear told himself, he's always been on the go, driving his Mercedes, peddling his watches, golfing, gambling, skiing, screwing. He must have a heart like a city pump.

Except for looks—a crumb off the muffin, thought Spear—red hair, blue eyes, small chin, stubbiness, no son seemed farther from a father than Timmy. He was as focused—by his band and songs—as his father was diffuse. Hugh was loose, prodigal; Timmy—as Spear saw him—was cautious, close, laconic, though in his quiet way a responder and smiler. Jennifer opened up around him, smiled into his smiles, even more at ease with him, thought Spear, than with Colin Morgan.

"Maybe it's cousinship," Spear told Hugh. "A built-in equality. Nobody has to put on airs. Not that she does much of that, but she's told me how tense she gets taking depositions or arguing in court. Timmy's such a nice chap. How's he doing?"

This as the four of them walked back to Jennifer's, the old cousins yards behind the two they were pushing together, although both sensed that there was something askew in the pairing. Even physically, the two didn't match. Jennifer was erect and inches taller; Timmy was a compact sloucher. They also sensed that within Timmy's affection for Jennifer there was a discomfort about her position and salary. Though he enjoyed doing what he did, and she didn't enjoy what she did, he seemed to register the world's contempt for his hand-to-mouth existence, its respect for her professionalism and routine.

"Damn well," said Hugh. "I haven't had to give him a nickel. He's got plenty of work, turns down jobs. He's thinking of buying a little house in San Rafael, just asked if I'd drive up tomorrow to look at it."

"I'll go along if you like. Fer's back at work, I've got nothing doing."

"I'd love it, but his car's a two-seater. Actually, I got the sense that he wants to ask me something. Probably money for the down payment. Which I'll gladly give him."

[13]

"Nothing to do with a down payment at all," said Hugh, two mornings later. He and Spear were dawdling over sausages and pancakes at a breakfast place on Columbus. Jennifer had gone off to the Embarcadero Center, and Timmy had driven down the peninsula for a gig in Palo Alto. "He didn't tell me what till we were on the Golden Gate. A year ago, after one of his concerts, he spent the night with a girl he'd never seen before, a groupie. He saw her a couple of other times, liked her well enough, but that was that. He got a letter or two from her, nothing pressing, just affection. A few weeks ago, he had a letter saying she thought he might like to know that she'd had his baby; she wasn't asking for money or marriage, but she thought he was entitled to know. If he wanted to see the baby, that was fine with her. If he didn't, that was fine too. So he went to see her. She lives in San Rafael, runs a bed-and-breakfast there. Anyway, that's whom we went to see, that's why he wanted only me to come.

She's a pretty, very able girl, and the baby's a beauty. Timmy's already crazy about him, and he likes the girl too. He's given her money; he intends to stick with her, be the baby's father."

"Astonishing. You have a grandchild."

"I have, yes. A beauty. Not a Wallace, but—who knows?"

"Will Timmy marry her?"

"He doesn't really know her. What he does know, he likes. She isn't asking one thing from him. She had to be talked into taking money from him."

"She lives off this bed-and-breakfast?"

"She had a couple of years at San Francisco State, some office management program, so what she does every now and then—it's temp work—is set up computer programs for small businesses, hardware stores, sports shops, florists. She can do it at home and take care of Stevie. Timmy could do worse."

"You did. Frequently." Spear pushed away his plate. The pancakes and sausages were churning his stomach.

Timmy Wallace was not going to father Spear's great-grandchildren. That was clear.

All through the day with Hugh, walking down to the wharves, looking at the seals nuzzling and shoving each other like drunken choirboys, or buying a mobile for little Stevie at Ghiradelli Square—poor exchange for the watch Hugh had given Jennifer—riding the cable car up to the Fairmont for tequila or, back at Jennifer's, playing gin with his usual crazy luck, he felt a knot of nausea in his stomach. Lucky in cards but not where it counted. Hugh had stumbled into his future, a Wallace in genes, if not name, whereas his Jennifer was dancing the *Catherinette*. What was going to become of her? Would she, like her grandfather—but thirty years prematurely—become a hermit? From boyhood on, bicycling alone on the moors, hunting for birds, Spear knew that he had an aptitude for solitude. When, with retirement and Vanessa's death, it had been thrust upon him, he'd been ready for it. Jennifer would be ravaged by it, embittered and stunned, far more than her mother was by—whatever. Jennifer was made to be with people, with companions, lovers, a husband. "Gin."

"You get a fortune," said Hugh. "Fifteen, nineteen, twenty-nine, forty-nine, fifty-two. And twenty-five for gin." He scribbled on the score pad.

"I'm schneidered. A hundred and fifty points. You win a fortune." They played for a quarter of a cent a point. "Nineteen dollars and seventy-five cents."

Spear loved gin triumphs over Hugh; not today. Even while he knew, rationally, that it was absurd, excessive, self-centered, stupidly old-fashioned, almost psychopathic, he couldn't shake off the vision of his wonderful granddaughter alone, a tiny island in the immense cold ocean of solitude.

[14]

One March Saturday, Jennifer walked down to the Exploratorium to hear her grandfather's love tape. It was the first Saturday in a long time she hadn't worked at least half a day or spent more than half of it with Jack Cole, the partner with whom she'd been sleeping the last three and a half months. (One of the few Saturdays she'd not spent with Jack, she'd spent with Colin Morgan, in town to take depositions. That was the second time she'd gone to bed with him, the first being when he'd driven down late Christmas Eve the night they'd met.)

The Exploratorium was full of families. Even the love tape section was crowded. Jennifer was in no hurry. That morning, she'd awakened thinking of her grandfather and, remembering the tape, was suddenly curious to hear and see it. While she waited in line, she put on headphones and listened to other tapes. The speakers were sentimental, inarticulate, dull. She drifted into her own tape (which she'd never make): the first time she'd made love, in high school, with Louis Fuzollo, the surprise and messiness of it; then the two months with Louis's cousin Michael; foggily she thought of the horrible eighth-week abortion her senior year, followed by months of depression—and abstinence—till, in Northampton, her first good relationship, sophomore year, with Henry Greif, her Western-Civ instructor. After that, her Slut-Time: she'd slept with a dozen boys from U. Mass. and Amherst who'd passed her around like a chain letter, but it was interesting, exciting, like a good miniseries full of plot turns and surprises. Junior year in Paris, she'd been relatively celibate: there was a month with Ling Tsien, a Singapore-Chinese at the Science Po' who wanted to marry her, then the bicycle tour through Gers to the Pyrenees, where she'd slept in a tent with Jean-Michel What's-his-name. In law school, there was no time for anything but bouts of sheer relief—"getting the ashes hauled"—sleeping with fellow sufferers, the most interesting, a first and probably last—Denise Solle, the blond *Law Review* editor. "A full dance card" was the phrase that came to her as she signed for Spear's tape.

[15]

A few days later in his cabin, Spear read Jennifer's letter, one which, had he heard it years ago in a film, he might have called—or mocked as—sentimental, but which now, reading and rereading, he found almost sublimely beautiful.

Dearest Grandpa,

This morning I went to the Exploratorium and saw your tape. It felt so odd to watch it with twenty other people listening to you while those waves rolled in behind your head on that Bach music. It didn't matter. Nothing mattered but you and what you said. I know too that there are all sorts of love in the world, and that the kind we have for each other is less intense than many. Still, I think that as long as I live, I will feel it and know that there's nothing else like it. You say that you've known it twenty-six years: so have I. Please God we'll know it twenty-six more, and more than that. I will, even if you're not with me in the flesh.

Sitting in the dark in front of the monitor with your face that I know so well talking to me, I felt very very lucky. Thank you so much for giving me this, for being the grandfather you are.

Always, your

Fer

★   ★   ★   ★

"Rose had arthritis, diabetes, rheumatism, never left the house. I'm out, always, Morton's, Monkey Bar, Fiji East. My girls like that. You're with 'em. We have clients you wouldn't believe. Sony, Viacom, Mobil, Fox Network, you name it. . . . Some clients don't know the score. Camille Weil wanted girls for her husband's bachelor party. At two hundred dollars apiece. I said, 'Sorry, Camille, do them yourself.' . . .

"I don't know who put the cop on me. I saw him eye me outside the Rangoon. An Oriental dude in a Testarossa. Everybody but me knew. He was at the Beverly Hilton—but you don't know. Some guys rent two floors there. He says, 'Can I pay with *pakalolo?*' [Hawaiian for "marijuana."] I say, 'No *pakalolo.* Strictly Ben Franklins.' I sent him Soo'in, Johnny R's ex. They found ten grams of coke on her. She was a jabber-jaw. The roof caved in.

"But I still got this [waves the red book]. *World Book of Ape Sleaze.* . . .

"I've had times with real gentlemen. Tony Schmidt. His pals think they're studs, getting it for free. Tony pays for everything. Joe Osman's kid went to Nassau. Tony said, 'Get him a girl.' The kid meets her, does her, marries her. Who can figure.

"I bet a coupla thousand on every Raider and Laker game. We had a party for the Bills, day before they play the Raiders. They got outta here at five A.M. I bet thirty grand against them. You know what? They won!

"Don't rely on anyone. . . .

"No bragging, but I think I can say I've accomplished more in one year than anyone ever has. Madame Rose took ten years to build her setup; I built mine in six months! No one can ever take that away from me."

From Becky Faule, in conversation with Rolf Stuppe,
Rebecca of Cunnybrook Farm (Knopf, 1994)

KENERET ★ The Shooter Shot

[1]

Thirty years ago, almost to the month, another rug had been publicly pulled out from under Keneret. He himself had been the rug puller, not indirectly, as was the case here, loss of confidence augmenting Duggan's slippery patronage. Then it had been in front of cameras, not world-wide—he'd been spared that gigantism of humiliation—but wide enough. (The eventual attention was worldwide, and for months, the mindless MGM clipping service sent him highlighted mentions of it from publications in Delhi and Dar es Salaam.)

It was Academy Awards night, the third time he'd attended that Bar-numania of self-advertisement. In those days, there was no ducking at-tendance, and he'd been nominated for *Unless It Die*. It was unusual to be nominated for your fourth film; he was considered a comer, and en-joyed it. Elizabeth, his wife of seven years, disapproved, of course, partly because she'd have to get dressed up, and though she did it austerely, with her special mark of classy bad taste, it went against what she didn't even like to think about as her grain. Still, it took but a minute to show her that it was part of what they were doing out here, which meant that it was her "duty," and for her, *duty* was a sacred word, related as it was to one she would never utter, *martyrdom*, and another, of which she was equally gun shy, *self-sacrifice*. Maybe he was unfair. These Elizabethan motifs came into existence when he *betrayed her*—the operative phrase—or, at least, when she became conscious of the betrayal. In a way he hadn't analyzed but believed, he'd never betrayed her: that is, after twenty years with Marcia, he still cared for, indeed—in some down-to-earth section of the ethereal continent Love—loved her. Elizabeth was modest, reliable, decent, good-humored—she had a wonderful laugh—and, in her spare, unglamorous way, very attractive. Another attraction: she had never really bought him (or anyone else). Early, she'd taken her stand against the tyranny she'd experienced growing up under the harsh words and calloused hand of Ruthie, a brilliant black housekeeper who, at seventeen, had been given to Elizabeth's mother as a wedding present. Ruthie's domestic tyranny was the spur of Elizabeth's independence.

In their marriage, she was housekeeper, wife, cook, laundress, shopper, gardener, mistress of all; and all had been more or less mastered. Her efficiency was deliberate, everything done with—to Keneret—maddening slowness. The pace countered his impatience and was another way his quiet wife preserved her independence.

Or so Keneret thought in the few times he'd thought about her character. Mostly he preferred to think that he didn't understand her. (The mystery was an attraction.) What she was didn't really matter to him. She smoothed much of his life; they got along; she attracted him; the household was pleasant; they agreed about politics—they were FDR liberals—and, usually, people. Together, they'd overcome small and large domestic difficulties. (After Elizabeth endured a painful late abortion, they agreed not to have children.) Nor did she try to understand him. He was there, a somewhat too large presence, the condition in which she existed. She coped with it, at least while she still cared for him; she enjoyed his humor and believed in his gift. This before she realized that he was mentally and sexually bored by her and slept with other women.

For the awards ceremony, Elizabeth had even bought a new dress, one so unstylish it reasserted her *je m'en foute* style. The studio supplied a chauffeured Lincoln which discharged them at the theater, where they

had their forty seconds under klieg lights before yielding to more cele-
brated celebrities.

During the tedious hours preceding the Best Director award, Keneret
sank away from the mind-boggling musical numbers, the parade of gorgeous guys and dolls, the droning technical awards, and the verbose
seizures of gratitude. Elizabeth shook him just in time to open his eyes
at his own nomination, but he was still half fogged when the envelope
was opened and the winner's name, Ken Rhodes, was announced. Hearing the first syllable of his own name, Keneret started down the aisle. Elizabeth reached for, then went after, him, but not before first ten, then a
hundred, and finally God knows how many hundreds in the auditorium
and millions elsewhere roared at his mistake. Rhodes hadn't seen him,
but Bob Hope, the slick MC, had and proclaimed, "I know, Ez, you can't
believe it. They've robbed me too for years."

The studio was delighted: Keneret had stolen the show and brought a
million dollars of free publicity to what had been a sinking film. They is-
sued the story that he, the forgetful genius, was rushing up to congratu-
late Rhodes.

Decades later, there were still people who remembered Keneret for
that mistake. It had been a national joke, and six months later, at a White
House reception, the president said to him that he thought he'd deserved
the award. "If you'd beaten him to the podium, maybe they'd have given
it to you." (Keneret did not relay this presidential opinion; the studio
would have spread it over the world.)

[2]

There'd been another rug pull, a catastrophe in slow motion. He'd made
a film called—with awful prescience—*The Unmaking of Janie*. Once
again he'd been riding high. The first three months' work was develop-
ment heaven: the transformation of book to script to storyboards was
dream smooth. They'd made the film for peanuts. (Duggan had worked
out the finances with brilliant parsimony: units sold to limited partners;
fees locked into completion bonds; distribution fees taken off the top;
special guild and union agreements with SAG and NABAT; DuArt's lab
work done under a partial deferment agreement; downsize protection

from videocassette and cable markets.) Even Keneret, famously finicky, finished principal photography in forty days and edited during production. They were all going to prosper. The film itself seemed as good as any he'd made. A rough cut was shown to festival organizers and distributors and went well. They had guaranteed play dates in a hundred and fifty markets. It would be a number-3 choice, after the latest blockbuster and "the one you missed." The first test market was the Seattle Film Festival, the second the Seventy-second Street Embassy in New York. The first week's gross at the Seattle Varsity was twelve thousand, at the Embassy, fifteen. *Village Voice* had a glitzy new Sarris clone who called it "weird and thrilling" and offered an explanation why Keneret's films weren't blockbusters. (Keneret put it on his bulletin board.)

> *They don't salve our irritation or reinforce our sluggishness, but puzzle and unsettle us. Their beauties and comforts aren't handed out on silver platters; an audience has to work a little, but this is the audience which insists that Keneret films get made.*

The crucial review, though, was the one in the *New York Times*. It sounded the pitch for Keneret fans, and many reviewers took their cue from it. Word of mouth was conditioned by it; and it spread out from New York like flu. In Keneret's mind, the *Times* was even more important. It was the newspaper he, his family, friends, and relatives read and had read much of their lives. Knock it, mock it, chide it, deride it, it was in the American scene like the White House, Harvard, Nobel Prizes, and the Bible. Keneret's films had made and lost millions because of single *Times* phrases. For decades, he'd been alert to its 2:00 A.M. edition, and, on review nights, his sister, Eileen, stayed up hours after her bedtime to buy and read it to him in California.

Before *The Unmaking of Janie* review, he'd spent days trying to lower expectations, but at 11:15, when the phone rang, he was tense as a drum.

"Ez dear, I don't think you want to hear it."

Awful pause. "Read it."

"It's not by Barnes. Some new reviewer, Sally Ba—"

"Read it, Eileen."

"There's a good sentence at the end."

"Eileen, please."
She read:

The Unmaking of Janie is like a cryptic text from the Dark Age of film. One keeps waiting for a scene, a speech, anything to explain its apparently willful obscurity, but no, the film clunks along ever more mysteriously. You begin to wonder if the film itself has been damaged, if the projectionist was drunk; anything rather than this charmless, hollow mess. Yes, hollow. The film's core is hollow, as if its old director had lost it en route to the studio. . . . The worst of it is its attempt at contemporaneity which is like the ill-made denture and toupee of a raddled grand dame. No Movie-of-the-Week could be stuffed so full of banality and misjudgment. There is only one sequence which isn't laughable: its three minutes seem spliced from another film.

Keneret's heart banged away so loudly he didn't hear all the words. Not necessary. It was clear. His film had been murdered.

Eileen said, "She's not reviewing it. She's out to make her career. She doesn't mention any of your other films. It's as if they don't exist. As if she's never heard of you."

"She doesn't want me to exist."

Eileen sobbed.

An icy splinter of Keneret thawed for his sister. "Don't worry, baby. It's so extreme, it cancels itself."

"I'm going to write. I'm going to get everybody to write the paper. I'll kill her."

"It's good for me. I was expecting to make a killing. I've never had anything good come of expectation. Every good thing in my life has been a surprise. So it bombs in New York."

"You have fans here. Thousands."

"A year's work. I'm sorry you had to see it. Sorry your friends will read it."

"My friends love every film you've ever made."

"Thank them for me."

"You're the one to be thanked. You've given them, me, wonderful wonderful hours."

He turned out the light and sat waiting to die. Sally B. was right. He'd lost it. But what about the opening shot on the bus? The crosscuts on the beach? Janie's seduction? They worked. He knew it. The test cards in Seattle were great. They loved it. Something was biting that New York bitch. There was something that got to her personally. What was it? Janie's passivity? But Janie wasn't really passive. The fucking bitch misunderstood her, misunderstood the film. She thought he was an old macho dinosaur and crushed him without watching the film. Hundreds of people, thousands of hours, down the toilet because a fucking ugly bitch had a bellyache.

Over the next two weeks, Marcia and Spear talked him out of the pit, and then Pauline Kael's review appeared in the *New Yorker*, no rave, but appreciative, discerning.

Yet the film bombed; the numbers never turned.

[3]

Driving back to Santa Monica from Bel Air, Keneret, soaked in despair, remembered it all. Here he was again, broken, empty. After *Janie*, Duggan had brought him back from film exile, from the grave of not working. Now he'd reburied him, as if Christ had raised Lazarus so he could throttle him.

"We gave it three weeks, Ez. We never liked it, but we went along because it was you. And the first rushes surprised us. They were fine. Even Scholem was surprised." Vlach didn't move, maybe a small nod. "He'd thought *Janie* was your swan song. Right, Scholem?" Another maybe-nod. "But this one . . . this one was just . . . too ambitious for its size. Just not enough there, Ez."

Said Vlach, "The sign of decline. Bertolucci, 1900. Griffith, *Intolerance*. Faulkner, *A Fable*. We regret, Ezra."

[4]

In the leather cocoon of his Porsche, Keneret gripped the scalloped wheel. The easy, sexy grip tonight felt like barbed wire. *He was through.* The excitements of preparation and shooting had briefly blotted that out.

The mansions of Bel Air and Beverly Hills certified his nothingness. The palms, the castle-heavy canyons, the loud stretch of money, hooted. Night gonged away.

His fifty-thousand-dollar hunk of metal hustled toward the ocean, missed the turnoff at Twenty-sixth for San Vincente, took Sunset to Ocean Drive, and turned, somberly, left. Sea air.

Duggan, Vlach. *Vaudevillians from hell.* He should've buttered the carpet in that Potemkin Library with their brains.

Sea air and black ocean didn't help. He drove home. At least that was there. It didn't know that there'd been an earthquake, that its master was falling through a fissure.

He sat in the car, ignition on for enough seconds to scare him. He turned it off and went into the street. His street. If anything was still his. Night. Stars. Houses. The air, a breeze; a hum. Maybe it's that effect: a UCLA geologist had told him that the earth contracted like a soft football every fifty-three minutes; the contraction produced a note, an E flat twenty-two octaves below middle C. "It's the heat waves moving in the planet's pipes." By the plastic ritual bush of baby shoes and scrolled prayers in front of the Iwinaga house, Keneret listened to the E flat.

"My swan song."

He debated, then, mockingly, angrily, discarded the idea of writing out a prayer for the bush.

[5]

Sunday. Home, with what was still his. Breakfast on the terrace, the bi-coastal compendia of the world's week at either end of the glass table, the *Times* of L.A., the *Times* of New York. "Why don't we get London's?" There were Oregon blueberries over his Swiss cereal, a rack of buttered cinnamon toast, silver urns of regular and decaffeinated coffee, a half grapefruit with a cherry for Marcia—Lourdes, the beautiful Filipino cook, scalloped the rind and sliced it so that the segments could be lift-ed without impediment—fresh mango juice for him.

An American king.

Dethroned.

He'd told Marcia when he'd come in. "I felt something awful would happen. I've been in a state." She'd held him till he said that he felt contagious and moved to the other side of their huge bed. Now he said, "I tell everybody tomorrow. The last payout. The last nickels Duggan spends on me."

The grapefruit was pushed away "How could Duggan have—?"

"It's in the 'could.' That he could is why he did."

Soulful, wistful, and—best—ignorant, Babette came in with a basket of hot biscuits; but she saw. "Something bad, Madame?"

"A little bad, Babette. Business. But you know, good times follow bad."

Babette's round, bright face turned cloudy. "You will not have to leave this house?"

The Kenerets looked at each other over the croissants and silver coffee urns, gauging this other level of apprehension.

"No, Babette. Nothing like that. And do not alarm Lourdes. There's nothing for either of you to worry about."

Babette exhaled deeply, then took the urns, one in each hand, and filled their cups, Keneret's first, the silver spout inches higher than usual as if relief had given her new energy and converted it into a virtuosity of service. Keneret watched the coffee plunge blackly into the blue-and-gold-rimmed cup as if he were framing it for a shot, then, remembering, pulled up short and broke the frame.

"Thank you," he said, and, when she'd left the terrace, "Strange what a few hours can do to a life. Everything feels cramped. No place to go. It's not visible, an outsider wouldn't notice anything, but everything's changed. Nothing belongs anymore," then, seeing Marcia's constricted face, "Lord God, not you. You're the lifeline. More than ever. The only one. Tomorrow everybody here will know I'm out. Every face will look different. They'll look through me. I'm not there anymore. Transparent. Empty. A nothing. What that writer Ellison said blacks felt in white streets. The visibility so threatening it has to be unseen. Oh, we're a species, we are. Why talk of savages? As if this"—arms spreading over the table toward the garden, the lemon tree, the honeysuckle, the lawn, the blue pool, the house, the French doors, the terrace, the silver urns— "transformed us. Inured us."

Marcia didn't interrupt. Her husband's aria was easing what it groaned about, but when it stopped, she was ready with salves: Ezra could take a course at UCLA. "Remember how you adored that Shakespeare course, how inspired you were?"

He remembered. "I'm not up to that now. The only part I'd understand is his going back home at forty-five to clip his coupons."

"Let's get out of here, then. Deluxe. Paris, the Ritz. Madrid, ditto. Anywhere, Bali, Bora Bora, Fiji." A mistake. "Oh, dear, sorry sweetheart."

"No, that's the point. I can't outrun this. Have to take it, not dodge it. Feel it, then maybe understand it, even, who knows, make something of it."

"But you don't have to do it here. I'm better not moving; you're better in motion," and in a bit she came up with a trip that seemed possible, away but not too far or difficult: Keneret had spent two-thirds of his life on the West Coast, he'd been on all the continents but Antarctica, but had not been to the Pacific Northwest, except a couple of days at the Seattle Film Festival.

"And you were upset because it rained and you couldn't see Mount Rainier. Fly up there, I'll stay here, in touch. Even drive up if you feel like it, that coast is so gorgeous. Thea Harmel has a place in Neskowin. You could spend the night there; you like Thea. You'd be as near as if you were in Century City, you could fly back in an hour, but I don't think you'll need to. You know what being gone even for a day is like for you. When you come back, everything seems new."

Keneret looked at this person of whom he never tired, never for more than a few seconds, a few minutes. Twenty-plus years now, and in the last ten or twelve, they'd learned how to live together almost without arguments. Amazing. A few times a year, one or the other would blow up, but then retreat, make peace. To have this shell of love, what luck. The world's Duggans couldn't take that away.

So he listened to her, his companion-physician, prescribing the prescription. As uncertain as a new drug, but he trusted the prescriber, itself a comfort. "I don't know if I can manage anything. I can hardly pee by myself."

"You don't have to do much more. I'll make the reservations, work everything out. And tomorrow, if you like, I'll go down with you to the studio. I guess I can't talk to the cast or crew, but I can be there and look as sorry as I feel." He shook his head. "Of course. You're the only one, and better alone."

"It's the last act of authority, almost something to relish. Maybe not, but I can manage it. They'll see we're in the same sinking boat."

Marcia understood her husband's quasi-religious need for self-abasement, self-contempt. Often she hated it, as she hated anyone who hurt or demeaned him, but it was part of what made him him, and what made his work so beautiful and appealing, far more moving to her than Harmel's brilliantly sensuous comedies. Spear's book on Ez's films described the confidence and depth of his modesty and showed how it helped form his films. Though it went against her own grain, she had come to accept that it was as much a part of him as his energy, decency, and talent, essential to the man whose love was the center of her life, if not her being.

[6]

At the Seattle-Tacoma Airport, Keneret picked up a small blue Lincoln, drove south and east to the freeway, then took 161 to Puyallup. Every once in a while he looked south and east for the snowy peak of Mount Rainier, but though it was a clear day, it was in hiding; either that or he was looking in the wrong place. He was surely getting closer. The road angled up; there were woods and, in the distance, other mountains.

In tiny Elbe, he bought a roast beef sandwich in the general store and ate it on a bench between a white church and an abandoned locomotive. Elbe.

Maybe this is where I was meant to go. Could I take it for a hundred days? Then what? Well, Napoleon picked up steam in Elba for one more go. Who knows? Cutting through a skirt of motels, then forest, he felt the tension of the last days seeping out of him.

At the Nisqually entrance to the park, he handed five dollars to the ranger and received his information packet. A little too much education, but then, except for the good road, marked trails, rangers, and a couple of inns, this was undoctored nature.

He felt grandly alone, no one to worry about or with, just himself, the

Lincoln, and the unsinister grandeur of giant trees. Every now and then, he pulled off on a crescent-shaped extension of the shoulder, turned off the motor, and walked toward them. Spruce, fir, ash, redwood. Starved for sunlight, they shot straight up, their grooves and groins ancient with rectitude. Keneret let something in himself rise along the grooves. The silence was deepened by the scuff of his shoes and the swish of small animals scooting in the underbrush. The air was so fresh it was a taste. I'll pack some, take it home. No, you don't rob cathedrals, and these grooved trunks were the best sort: no orthodoxy pressure from them.

The car took the curves slowly, as if it, too, enjoyed its power. Rounding another curve, he saw an enormous broken slab of white springing out of a hole in the clouds and nearly went off the shoulder. Another curve, and it was gone, still another, and it burst out at him again.

The monster. The mountain.

Ten minutes later, the sun out, he saw its enormity, flat and peaked, conical and round, a complexity of immensity, somehow one thing.

[7]

The lodge was long, timbered, steep roofed, chimneyed. Keneret carried his bag into a high-planked lobby and signed in.

His room was a bed, a sink, a closet; the toilet was down the hall. Outside the small window sat the mountain, staring indifferently at him. Framed in the window, remote, a mass of untouchability. How could anyone dream of climbing it?

Maybe he'd try a few yards on one of the trails.

Twenty minutes later, in boots, sweater, and jeans, he crossed the road and started up, managing a hundred inclined yards before he felt it in his chest. Whew. He tried one step at a time, this he could manage, and when he felt the tightness again, he held up and studied bushes, vines, trees. Even on this instep of the mountain, the air was wonderful. And the flowers, purple, scarlet, gold, darling things peeking out of clumps of bronze shrubbery. High up, the gleaming flattop invited the blue sky. Was it Cézanne who had gone out every day for years and years to paint a mountain, so involved with it he missed his father's funeral? His mountain. His *motif*. His job.

More steps, more breath; a bird, red winged, white breasted, snooty, looking at him from a blueberry bush. *Salut, oiseau.* It lifted very large wings and—*off.* Keneret watched it become a piece of nothing.

[8]

Alone by a window that gave on the blueberry bushes from which he'd looked down, Keneret drank red wine before, during, and after fish soup, beef, potatoes, asparagus, salad, rolls, apple tart, and ice cream. Thinking of sleep, he abstained from coffee.

From a public phone in the lobby, he called Marcia, cupping the speaker away from the inquisitive phone-waiter behind him, then, on the verandah, sat with smokers and watched the mountain turn into shadow. The moon squatted on it. A bird, eagle or hawk, flew in on a blade of moonlight, then off until it turned into dark. Keneret, alone now, was cold. Getting up, he felt a gush of acid in his throat, burning, and then, as if it had been shot, his stomach cramped. He sat down hard on a bench, sweat pouring down his face, soaking his shirt. Freezing, immobile, he felt a brick form in his stomach. He rubbed there, round and round, pressing for relief. His chest was tight, his breath short, the brick immovable. *I'm going to have to get help,* but a few minutes' rubbing in the dark eased him enough so that he could get up and—though bent over—move as if looking for something dropped. He made it into the lobby, bent, humiliated, inching his way. In the corridor was a bathroom into which he managed to stumble and sit, dense with cold sweat, trying to evacuate the brick. Finally, painfully, something gave, and with partial relief, he got to the staircase and pulled himself by the banister to the second floor and his bed.

He knew that he'd have to vomit before he could sleep. After gathering some strength, he bent over the toilet bowl. Throat harsh with acid, he worked to cough out the brick. He got out bits, some relief, rinsed his mouth and got back to bed. Back and forth, bed to bowl, he went for hours until, after midnight, he had the crucial heave.

Brick gone, stomach soft, relief. Weak but joyous, he turned over and slept for eight hours.

★　　★　　★　　★

Every history has a history. This riot didn't start with the Not Guilty in Simi Valley. Where you start depends on what you're after: West African villages if you want to blame the greed of slavers and African chiefs. . . .

When the *maquillistas* are sweat-shopping rage as well as jeans and silicon chips—the wafers of the Information Church—you get the despair we got back in Fontana when Kaiser Steel was broken by Detroit and New York finance. The kids and grandkids of the Okies lost not just their paychecks, bungalows, and pools but their California souls. . . .

You shouldn't be interviewing me. I'm just a *chispa* of the old Wobblies' fire, a worn-out old Leninist sticking to old guns. Interview these kids from San Bernadino and Riverside who came down to Parker Center to be with each other, Asian kids, Mexican kids, black kids, Wasp kids like me. It was love, not riot. Interview the kids and ex-kids and kids who never were kids at Florence and Normandie. Or Watts. Talk to the kids in the *clicas,* not to me. I'm just a pen-soldier in the Carey McWilliams–Louis Adamic–Mike Davis army doing my basic training in the archives, the newspaper morgues, the streets. . . .

I came to L.A. in '64, the year Ed Kienholz chopped a '38 Dodge, put it in Lover's Lane, turned on the car radio, and arranged a dead couple into missionary position in the front seat. The County Supervisor wanted to shut down the County Museum. If I can do a Kienholz here and there, I've earned my wages. . . .

From an interview with Danny Hanks Chisholm,
Fresno Free-Press, February 18, 1993

LEET ★ A New Way

[1]

When Leet is asked when things turned around for her, she says, "They're still turning." Her firm, HAL, Inc., is in the business of describing careers, but Leet is cautious about describing her own. She says that there have been different clocks in her life.

"In the village, it hardly ticked. You picked berries, you fetched the cows, you biked to Monsieur Chermineau's for bread so hot you couldn't hold it in your hands, you biked to the market in Meillac, you played football—our football—you read, sewed, went to school, talked with Hélène, Felice, Georginette. And Papa's visits—that's what they were— and you didn't know when they would be. After the letter that we were to forget him, something happened to the clock. I think that clock's still running me, as if the hands never finished going around the dial, but there've been other clocks, the one for *collège* in Tarbes and failing the *bachot*, another for tennis, the tournament, then the ad in *Figaro*, the call to Vienna, getting the passport, going to Paris, and the flight to Sydney and Fiji. So fast, dizzy. The slow clock in Fiji, slower than the one in the village. Then Ezra Keneret came, and the clock blew up. I fell out of time till that day on the soundstage when he told us it was all over, the backer had pulled out, the picture was finished. I went back to my room, as frightened as I'd been when Mama read us the letter from Argentina, but alone. I didn't leave the room for three days, but then I got back my job in the deli. I was so happy when Mr. Linsky took me back. I was at home there; I knew the language of pastrami and being hit on. Back in the room, though, it was hard. I kept thinking that what happened to the film was what happened with Papa. Because it was his story, it had happened again, and I thought I'd never get away from it.

"Then Dillon came into the deli. I hadn't seen him since that day on the soundstage. I thought it was an accident, but he came back that night and the next day. A week later, I moved into the Westholm with him."

[2]

Dillon was simple, gentle, and said almost nothing. Stupid? Leet thought not. He'd grown up in foster homes, in one of which he heard little more than *Eat up* and *Shut up*. She learned to understand what was under the little he did say. He didn't learn from books, newspapers, or even his surroundings. She'd never seen anyone so insensitive to most of what was around, at least so incapable of describing it. He'd ask her the meaning of events—"What's that sound truck making noise about?" "I think it has something to do with the election"—and what she thought were ordinary English phrases.

"What's 'beatin' around the bush' mean?"

"I have no idea." She wrote it down, asked Mr. Linsky or Mrs. Marcus, the cashier, and told Dillon later. (He often forgot he'd asked her.)

The one thing Dillon did read with understanding was scripts, though with these too he sometimes asked for help. "What does 'Keep it under your hat' mean?"

He also understood what he'd seen and heard on the set. Indeed, over his seventeen film years, he'd become a thesaurus of Hollywood phrases: "I Concorded to London for a stand-up with a bunch of Judys, see if we chemistried."

Leet found the vocabulary ugly and chauvinist: "Her ass was a water-melon; Johnny wanted raspberries." "You could see light bouncing off her implants." His feelings weren't involved in the ugliness; the words came out of the world he knew, equivalent responses to the questions: *What was her ass like? What were her tits like?*

Leet found a sweetness in his battlement, a kind of intelligence in his minimal registration of feeling. It was as if she were the camera which turned it into emotional depth. Whatever made Dillon a movie star also made him Leet's lover. In the bad days, after the breakup of the film, he lifted her spirits. He was a wonderful lover, as if he'd reserved for touch a sensitivity deadened almost everywhere else.

"We're gonna shoot in Leimert Park tomorrow," he said. "I lived there once. With the Hinojoses. Good Spic people. Real nice to me."

"Where's Leimert Park?"

"Dunno. Never been back." Then, sensing her curiosity, "It's little houses, stores, black people. I was ten, eleven. It's probably changed. You wanna come? It's an early shoot. They want the sun coming up."

"Thank you, *chèri*," stroking the famous, square, slightly pouting, puzzled face. "Tomorrow I sleep and shop." She'd given up the deli.

"They got a Spic gang to patrol. Rooftops. So they don't throw stones on us."

"What's your character like?" Leet talked over his parts with him, her scheme to deepen his responsiveness.

"The usual."

"What's that?"

"A goof-off. I wear bangles, like I'm in a gang."

"Do you need to prepare?"

"I just read the lines."

"Sure," said Leet. "Like Brando." She knew that he'd memorized them and felt them the way a good conductor feels a score in his hands. Nothing to do: between Dillon's gift and his ability—or willingness—to talk about it was a gulf, just as there was between his tactile tenderness and his wordless lovemaking. There was no point asking a flower to explain itself.

[3]

Tired of idleness, Leet took on a secretarial stint with Wendell Spear, whom she'd met at the Kenerets. He asked her to take dictation for the book he was writing on Keneret's films.

"I'll go very slowly. I can see how sensitive you are, not just to language. That's more important to me than getting some mechanically perfect stenographer. Besides, you know Ezra. You'll be able to give me another slant on him." And, watching her face, "S-l-a-n-t, a different view, another angle of vision. Like a different camera angle. Don't worry. Anytime you can't follow something, speak up, I'll repeat it, explain it, spell it out. I'm in no rush."

Leet had a wonderful time with him. He was so patient, she learned so much, and the cabin was beautiful. It was very quiet in the canyon, a bit like Meillac, and driving up every morning in one of Dillon's Porsches was inexplicably moving to her. Inexplicable, till she realized how much working with Spear was, somehow, like being with Papa. The comfort of this was reinforced by talking about Keneret and his work, for he, too, especially after the collapse of the picture, had become paternally dear to her. (She and Spear, separately and together, visited him in the hospital where he'd had stomach surgery days after his return from Mount Rainier.) Nothing moved Leet more than the decline and failure of old men.

Her first hour at Spear's, they sat out on the terrace. The little lawn was full of white blossoms. "Big-pod caenothus," said Spear, putting a handful in her hand.

"The air is so fine here. And the birds, trees, flowers. I love it, Mr. Spear."

"See that hummingbird dipping into the blue bottle? I fill it with sugar water. My wife taught me years ago. When she stopped doing it, the birds left. Now they're back. Like me."

"Ahh, *je l'adore*, Mr. Spear. It's paradise up here."

"If you can take mudslides, fires, and occasional earthquakes. Look up, see that?"

"Yes, what is it?"

"Our national *oiseau*, a golden eagle. Come." He led her over the small flagstone terrace through a French window. "Here's where we'll work."

So it began, the daily drive, starting at 10:00 A.M. — "I don't want you stuck in traffic" — dictation till noon, then sandwiches and coffee made from several kinds of beans, which Spear ground himself. After lunch, Leet napped on a couch while Spear studied his notes and looked at clips on his Movieola. Then they started again. At 4:00, they stopped so she could beat the rush hour home.

When the book was finished, Spear recommended her for a job, writing the history of a friend's small company. It was the first time she'd written anything but a letter in English, but working for Spear had given her confidence. It was also the first time in her life that she'd saved money. Paid eighty-five hundred dollars for the history, she saved more than half of it. (At Dillon's, she paid no rent.) When she finished — it had taken her five months — she knew how to write English nearly as well as talk it.

"How can I get more such jobs?" she asked Spear. "I like this work. Reading records, old newspapers, looking things up in libraries. If I was smarter, I'd like to be a student of history."

"If you were any smarter, someone would be writing a history of you."

"That would take volumes."

"Put ads in trade papers. I think there are many companies around here that might like their histories written. I think that you'll get lots of responses."

She didn't. Big companies had their own researchers; smaller ones seldom thought of self-commemoration or couldn't afford hers.

Money running low — for she was now in her own apartment and wouldn't ask Dillon or anyone else for a loan — Leet invested in two ads, one in a legal, the other in an electrical supplies, magazine. Each hooked a client. Meanwhile, indirectly through Keneret, she'd found a roommate, a UCLA graduate student in Romance languages, Agnes Desoger, a friend of Sylvan Harmel.

The electrical supply store had been started by a grandfather whose grandson wanted a book to mark the former's retirement. The text was minimal and took her less than a month to write.

The law firm was small and fifty years old. It wanted character sketches of the twenty-five lawyers who'd been partners. It came to almost three hundred pages. Leet's fee was fifteen thousand dollars, a fee which, into her third month on the project, she wished she'd doubled. "Yet," as she told Agnes, "it's a real book."

Three more fish had taken the commemorative hook. Leet groaned. "What am I going to do?"

Said Agnes, "Show me the ropes. I'll write one of them. We can split the fee. If the third one's impatient, I know a friend of Sylvan's brother who can help."

This turned out to be Hypatia Kovic, a Croatian photographer Oscar Harmel had met on safari in Kenya. (Hypatia would become the *H* of HAL, Inc. Agnes was the *A*, and Leet, its founder-president, the *L*.)

[4]

Leet relished having such a bright, learned, spunky, independent, and amusing person as Agnes around. Also, it halved the rent, the phone, the gas, the chores, and the gloom of solitude: Dillon was on a two-month shoot in the Philippines. In any event, Leet had decided to break from him. Tenderness and lovemaking did not compensate for the monotony of their life. Dillon's mental subway, the slowest of trains, stopped at too few stations. Shy of scandal reporters and photographers, he went out only for the most carefully arranged publicity events; and he read nothing but scripts. On television, he watched only sports. Leet began to feel not just baffled and annoyed but doomed by him. Except for passionate and tender half hours in bed and vividly impassive ones captured by the camera, Dillon's existence was a sort of nonpathological autism. Leet had stopped trying to interpret his grunts, then had stopped living with him. ("His clock hardly moved.") What took his place—and more than that— were the work and the company that crystallized around and advanced it.

Leet saw Agnes's room fill with photographs of actresses, most of them scissored from newspapers and Scotch-taped to the walls. Agnes's favorites were Ellen Barkin, Jodie Foster, Natassja Kinski, Winona Ryder, and Uma Thurman. First, there were a dozen photographs, then thirty, and, in a few weeks, a hundred of them. Agnes asked her one evening for an assessment.

"What do you think of them apples?" The apples were Jodie Foster's. She posed in a black Armani suit, almost-bared breasts facing the camera, eyes, nose, and perfectly toothed smile tilted starward.

"Your favorite?"

"You can say that. Didja see *Hotel New Hampshire?*" Leet shook her head. *"Siesta?* Where she rubs Ellen Barkin's thigh till some creep breaks in and Jodie fucks him instead. Though she and Ellen do kiss. Didja see *Freaky Friday?*"

"I haven't seen movies since I'm here. *Sauf, de temps en temps, sur le tele.*"

"I'll take you to *Silence of the Lambs.* You'd like each other. She went to a French school, speaks *français couramment.* Now she's thirty and trying to look innocent. She's worked on her gorgeous little bod and wants to show it so she makes this stinker *Nell,* 'bride of Forrest Gump.' Then *Maverick* to show her little tits and some bummer about a prodigy to explain her own genius. I think my Jodie's messed up, running away from the likes of me. If only I could get to her."

"Good luck, but I'm not that way, Agnes."

"You never know."

"I think I know."

"I'm not going to lobby you."

"Lobby?"

"Persuade you. If you change your mind, here I am."

"Does it derange you that we're together, and I don't feel the same way?"

"Disturb me? A little. You're a beautiful woman. I like you. It'd be a drag if I loved you. Or if we just lusted for each other. The offer's on the books, but I won't make it again. Friends." She stuck out her hard palm. Leet, moved, kissed her cheeks.

From then on, they were perfect roommates. The four or five times a month that Agnes brought girls or, several times, Sylvan Harmel home, Leet stayed out of the way. If there were meetings at the icebox or the toilet, she was friendly and detached, though once, she and Sylvan, running into each other half naked, laughed, then, suddenly and passionately, kissed.

★　★　★　★

The Abused and Ignored

Pigeon. Fourteen-year-old girl from middle-class home in Kirksville, Mo. Thin, hollow cheeked, green eyed, hair dyed purple, mohawk cut, wears silver ring in nose, combat boots, red T-shirt on which is written in white marker letters DON'T HURT ME. Left home "because everybody picked on everybody," taking money from Mother's purse and Father's wallet. With three hundred dollars and knapsack (jeans, panties, soap, toothpaste, toothbrush, scissors, jar of Skippy peanut butter, six cans of StarKist tuna), took bus to L.A., walked the Strip, chased off by local prostitutes. She wore jeans cut off at the knees, put on lipstick, and made her first score, a sixty-year-old man in a Buick LeSabre who drove her to a motel room. He dropped two tens on the bed. Pigeon: "When he dropped his pants, I started crying. He got upset, asked me to stop, and walked out, saying he couldn't do it with a crybaby. I got a hold of myself, went back out on the street, and found a working-type guy. I said up front, 'Fifty bucks.' After that, it was easy. Loads better than living at home."

Pigeon's home is an abandoned building with boarded-up windows, bathtub, and toilet filled with human waste; the smell is unbearable. It's dark. She sleeps on a foul mattress. Five adolescents—twelve to sixteen—share this dwelling. "Two of 'em are tweakers," says Pigeon. ("Tweakers" is their word for speed freaks.) "They crawl along the floor through the garbage looking for drugs." Roxanne, thirteen, carries a metal bar with which she hits the wall as she lurches along. No one knows where she's from. Manolo is a tiny boy from Phoenix. There are two long scars on his left wrist, one recent. "I'll do it right someday." Not today. "Today is a good day." He's made ninety-two dollars, has come back with red wine, cigarettes, and pizza.

They talk of trying heroin tonight.

Excerpt from the 1994 *Report of the Los Angeles Commission on Runaways and Street Youth*, section IIa

JENNIFER ★ Downsized

A year before the fire that incinerated his house, Spear telephoned Jennifer in San Francisco to inquire about her Christmas plans.

"What's up, Grandpa?" Jennifer's voice, Dietrich rough in the lower register, hearing his, rose, Spear thought with pleasure rather than alarm. "You all right?"

"As rain. Thinking about Christmas and if you had plans."

"Plans?"

"St. Louis? Tahiti? Wherever?"

"Can't afford it."

A surprise. Unlike her grandfather, Jennifer never complained about money. He didn't know what she made now, hadn't asked since she told him a year or so ago, but in her third year as an associate with Schmidt, Barczyk & Cole, she must be doing pretty well. She'd moved to a fine apartment ten floors up on Greenwich and Hyde, she looked to him like a *Vogue* model, and drove a Riviera spiffier than any car he'd owned.

"Did you make a bad investment? Or"—shivering a bit—"is there some trouble?"

A pause in which Spear felt a gear shift in his breath and pulse. "Not really, Grandpa."

Alone in the Malibu canyon cabin, Spear felt himself reaching through the wires for his granddaughter's face. "Please tell me, if you can."

"Not exactly trouble." The voice was rougher now. "I don't have a job."

"You resigned?"

"They fired me."

"No. How could they?" The words felt like lead; he could hardly hoist them from his throat. "Y-you were doing w-w-wonderfully. How c-c-c-could they?"

"Didn't seem too difficult for them."

"Did something happen? An argument?"

"The recession happened."

"Yes, but for lawyers?" Spear put his hand around a glass of Scotch he'd poured for the phone call.

"Whole firms are closing, Grandpa. In our building alone, fifty lawyers, at least. With us, only the associates; the nine of us who came three years ago. We're all out."

"W-w-what exactly h-happened?"

"You know those environmental cases I worked on? Modesto Insurance. Our—their!—biggest client. It dropped us. *Them!*"

"N-not because of you?"

"I hope not."

"How long—w-when was this?"

"They dropped us in April. I was fired in June."

Spear put down the glass and counted on his fingers. "Four months. Is that it?"

"I got three months' separation pay. In a way, it's been grand. I took that trip to Glacier Park."

"Yes. But you didn't tell me what happened."

"I thought I'd get a job before I told anyone."

"You w-w-were dear to s-s-spare me. W-w-when there's—when you're in trouble, I w-want to know."

Even as he said this, Spear felt a dizzying whiff of fear. For Jennifer, for himself. He saw her in the air falling: this wonder to whom, by the mysteries of desire and protein, he was indissolubly connected. Her security was a crucial part of his. It was he who'd encouraged her to go east to school, then west to law school. (He'd paid for a part of both.) When she passed the bar on her first try, then got the job with Schmidt, Barczyk & Cole, he'd felt more pride and joy than for anything he'd ever done on his own. When he saw her name cut in black letters—MS. ABARBANEL—on the brass plate outside her cubicle on the twenty-fourth floor of 2 Embarcadero Center, he'd told himself that he had finally arrived; it was the end of his emigration: his second-generation American granddaughter belonged to the American establishment. Spear, who'd grown up hating the exclusions and cozy confidence of a class system which survived wars, revolutions, and the satiric fury of Anglo-Celtic genius to infect so much English life, felt nothing incongruous in this satisfaction. Now, out of the awful blue, this rude, crude economic expulsion.

Twenty years of school, every sort of lesson, camp, and special training, and here she was, the wonderful sum of that, the flower of the Spears, his darling granddaughter, dropped into the void. He managed, "I'm here for you, Fer. This place is here for you. Y-you can look for j-jobs down here. I'll speak to Ez Keneret. He knows plenty of l-lawyers. Ira Stein, one of the biggest. He'll die to get a brilliant young woman like you."

"Grandpa, Grandpa."

Spear wasn't quite sure what he'd said. Was it too much? Was he interfering, the way her mother interfered and thought he did? "F-f-forgive me, darling, I'm just d-digesting the news. But Fer, I do have p-p-people I can c-call."

"Thank you, Grandpa. I am having interviews. It's going to be all right."

"That's s-s-splendid." Some relief, but wasn't it there because she'd again wanted to spare him?

After he hung up, he got out his checkbook. He had to show her he was substantially there for her. Five hundred? No, that was no longer a significant sum. A thousand? That's what he used to give her for Christmas. This had to be special. Two thousand? Twenty-five hundred? He couldn't keep sending that unless—the image of Mr. Whipp flashed in

him—it was deductible. Still, deduction or not, this was time for a dec-
laration, a sign that something solid was there for her.

He wrote out the four figures, subtracted the total from his careful bal-
ance and put it in an envelope with a short letter. "Fer, dear—A few dollars to make me feel that I can help a little—Love, Grandpa." He walked
out to the road, stuck the envelope in the mailbox, and raised its red tin
flag. He felt better, a bit, he thought, the way astronauts might when the
booster drops away and the capsule heads into orbit.

[2]

After Jack Cole told her that they'd lost Modesto Insurance and two other
clients and had to let her go, Jennifer sat for an hour, phone in lap, pressing number buttons, then DISCONNECT, over and over, calling, then not
calling, friends, parents, Grandpa. She packed up and walked home
down Clay, Montgomery, and Columbus, an hour's good walk, clearing
her head.

Home, she opened her best bottle of wine, a 1985 Bordeaux *rouge*,
filled her tallest, prettiest wineglass, turned out the lights, and sat by the
window overlooking the Bay Bridge. Complicated liquid on her tongue
and in her throat, fingers enjoying the braided gold rim, breasts against
the flannel of her pj's, leather chair at her bottom, Jennifer took in the
night lights popping on in the city, making soft triangles of the bridge.
Still hers. Her apartment. Her chair. Her city. Her self.

That first hour, she hated Jack Cole as she couldn't remember hating
anyone in her life. The frigid, phony sympathy of the ex-lover–hatchet
man drilled a hole in her system out of which gushed hatred for her electronic cubicle: fax, phone, printer, processor, the Mac, the monitor, the
shelf of casebooks; for law itself; and for Modesto Insurance, which covered the ugly ass of corporate defilement; for Schmidt, Barzyck & Cole,
which covered the coverer; and, finally, for California, may it quake into
dust and havoc. She'd poured her mind, energy, hopes, and time down
an electronic sewer. Jack's forehead wrinkled into his stupid crew cut, his
chow nose with the hairy nostrils clashed with his absurd little bulldog
jaw. She hated him, yet . . . yet telling her hadn't been a picnic for him.
Firing her didn't give him pleasure. And face-to-face was better than find-

ing a letter from the managing partner in her pay envelope. For Jennifer, hatred wasn't easy.

Three years of—if not praise, approval. No associate in a good law firm expected more than that. Money was your praise. And it was a lot more money than she'd ever had.

Now she went through what she did have: three CDs (two for five, one for eight thousand), six thousand in her Bank of America checking account, two Vanguard funds. Enough for rent, groceries, and running her car for—what? Eight months? Ten? Better: she'd be getting twelve weeks' separation pay; and there was unemployment, however much that was. Sitting—more or less—pretty.

A river of car lights on the bridge; below, the clank and jangle of the cable car. Fer's in Frisco, not all's bad with the world.

Tomorrow—and every day—she could sleep as long as she wanted. She could bike, shop, walk, read novels, drink hot chocolate in Ghiradelli Square, go to the Kabuki Cineplex; she could meet nonlawyers, have dates. (That old word from Mama's generation. But she could not tell Mama, or she'd be out here with a van, trying to pack her up to take back to St. Louis.) Maybe she'd drive up the coast to Olympia Park, or take a cruise. That's how you meet people, isn't it? Handsome companions in white pants on white boats. Or Paris. Rome. They might be deductible. (Remembering Grandpa's strange auditor: "I was job hunting over there, sir.")

For the first time in a long time, she had time.

No more depositional battles, jurisdictional confrontations, hair-splitting debates about responsibility for poisoning what was left of the livable earth. No more dragging her bones home at midnight and rolling them out of bed at quarter of six, showering in thirty seconds, gobbling a croissant as she ran downhill to catch the bus. No more of the tension that constipated her for weeks.

She'd take care of herself, sleep half the day, cook up a storm, play tennis at the Alice Marble Courts, which she could see from her window but where she'd played only twice in three years. At her leisure, when she felt like it, she'd glance at the ads in the law journals.

By the time, four months later, that she told her grandfather, Jennifer had had two interviews, one with the brother of a girl she'd met in Glac-

ier Park, a fund-raiser for the Episcopal Church, the second with the
uncle of Shari Morgan. The uncle owned an audio-equipment company
in San José and was thinking of hiring in-house counsel. She was asked
back for a second round of interviews, but not only did the job pay much
less than what she'd earned at Schmidt, Barczyk & Cole, it didn't interest her. Maybe she wasn't ready to be interested. Leisure was still pleasant; and she still had money.

A week after she'd refused the second invitation to San José, the
droplets of panic she'd felt intermittently since April became a stream of
tension. Cycling, shopping, reading, going to dinner, the movies, or even
to bed with one of the men she ran into here and there, she felt head-
and stomachaches, which, she realized after she'd slept through them,
were in the panic stream.

Grandpa's check diverted the stream, then deepened it. For three
years, she'd earned as much, maybe more, money than he and as much
as her father. She was proud of that, in itself, and what it did for her sense
that she'd broken from the cocoon of dependence. It was the generosity
of the check that panicked her: Did she seem so needy?

Ten days after it arrived, she'd gone down to the State Building on
Turk Street and filled out the forms for unemployment compensation.
The insouciant ugliness of the rooms and corridors almost drove her away,
but the elderly black woman who interviewed her—"What sort of position are you looking for, Ms. Abarbanel?"—was so gentle and sympathetic
that it made acceptance of state money a natural, almost a patriotic, act.

Every two weeks then, a check for $467 arrived in an official envelope.
(If another tenant was at the lobby mailbox, Jennifer concealed it. Why
upset fellow tenants with what they paid money to hide from?) The day
she got her second check, she rewrote her resumé and sent it out with a
hundred and fifty computer-generated letters of inquiry to which, over
the next month, she received sixty-five answers, all but three politely negative. Of the three, two were for in-house counsel, one in San Rafael, the
other with an educational testing service in Mountain View. She drove
down to Mountain View for a second round of interviews and was con-
sidering their offer—despite a salary half what she'd made at SB&C—
until the vice-president, an amusing, gray-haired man whose walls were

covered with children's pictures, asked if she'd go with him to a jazz concert in Monterey.

The third letter was from Angela Persill, another SB&C firee. Angela was starting a practice with a few lawyers. "None over forty. Specializing in employment rights. Down our alley, Jen." Each lawyer had to put in twenty thousand dollars for start-up costs.

"That lets me out," said Jennifer.

"Borrow. Take our prospectus to the bank, I don't think you'll have a problem."

"Except for law school, I've never borrowed anything. Even borrowing from family threw me."

"Family! Luck-ee!"

"Maybe."

"Look here, Jen, I've got more to lose than you. It's exciting."

"I'm no good with risk, Angela. Probably the way I grew up, under the suburban gods: Security and Don't Take Chances." She didn't like being called Jen. She hardly knew Angela: they'd done one deposition together, just enough to let her see that frail Angela was one tough cookie. "I'm not entrepreneurial."

"You don't have to be. I am. I'm sure we'd work well together, like we did on that depo. I need a first-rate woman. We got two guys on board, one you know, Sid McSharoy." A no-brow, rat-eyed fellow Jennifer danced with at SB&C Christmas parties. "Rainmakers. But they make me uneasy; I don't want to get too male heavy."

"I would counter that."

"So would a lot of women. It's you I want. I'm so sure, I'll cover you for five, six thousand. If you can come up with the rest." A pause. "Am I pushing too hard?"

One hundred forty-seven doors had slammed in Jennifer's face. Angela's need for her, her ability, as well as her gender, felt good. Ten o'clock, a weekday October morning, she was still in pajamas; Angela had probably been up since six. "I appreciate this, Angela. The confidence. I've been losing mine. Can you let me think it out awhile?"

"Ab-so-lute-ly. Take two—three days. I'll hold off. You did a hell of a job on that depo."

"You had to straighten me out."

"You were good."

"But if I come in, I come in like everybody. I can get the money."

Lowering the receiver into its cradle, she knew that she wouldn't join Angela: even on the phone, she made her tense. But knowing that made her feel hollow.

[3]

Hollow was how Spear felt many times in the weeks after that first call. In subsequent weeks, Jennifer sounded, perhaps was, cheerful, but whatever else they talked about, he thought of little else but her situation and always came round to it. "Anything on the horizon, dear?"

"A few things, Grandpa. Nothing sensational."

"I spoke to Ez Keneret and Ira Stein. They'll ask around. Ira said he'd be glad to talk with you when you come down to L.A."

"That's nice, Grandpa. Thank you."

"I still don't get it. The market's in good shape. I'm worth more each month, at least on paper. What's going on?"

"You must only read the arts and feature sections."

"The obits, too. Why?"

"Check out page one. You'll see reductions in force, downsizings, bases closing, plants closing. The end of the Cold War hasn't been too great for California."

"So that makes you a casualty. Which makes me one."

"No, Grandpa, neither you nor I. I'm fine. You too."

The next day, he sent her a check for a thousand dollars.

"Dear Grandpa," she wrote back,

> I'm so grateful for the check, and I'm going to accept it as your Christmas gift, but you mustn't send any more. If I need money, I'll ask.
>
> There are jobs out there, I've just been finicky. I probably picked places I knew couldn't use me. I'll be buckling down real soon. Meanwhile, your too generous check will help pay my December rent.
>
> I haven't decided anything about Xmas. If I go home, there'll be a pitch to have me stay. You know how Mom hates California. She has

nightmares of me falling into boiling lava! I did finally tell her what was going on. After the first shock, she sounded happy. "Now you can come home." She told me last week she'd contacted nine lawyers, all of whom agreed to see me. Agreed!! They'd probably give a thousand dollars to get her off the phone. Maybe in a week or two, we can talk about Xmas. At the moment, except for your check, I don't have much Christmas spirit and I don't want to dampen yours. In any case, I'll be fine by myself and hope you will be as well.

Much love,

Fer

★　　★　　★　　★

The interview with Joe Pittman took place Saturday morning, January 30, 1994, almost two weeks after the 6.6-Richter quake, epicentered in Northridge, twenty-odd miles northwest of Pittman's little stucco house with its armed response sign just visible in the front-yard weeds. Pittman, a smallish, thinnish, sharp-faced man with ash-gray hair and strabismic brown eyes, lives here with his wife, Lois, and Mickey, a white pit bull. We drink coffee in the small kitchen. I ask him to sign my copy of Shitfaced Angels, *his classic book on L.A., published in 1990 by the Espresso Press.*

JP: I've signed too many things. Forgive me.

INTERVIEWER: I understand. It's total bourgeois property enhancement.

JP [*shrugging it off*]: Look, everybody but those who live here loves the idea of L.A. being burned to the ground, leveled by earthquakes. Catastrophes. California is more menaced than any place but maybe Bangladesh. Maybe 'cause we're not one place. We're six.

INTERVIEWER: Spell that out.

JP [*using fingers*]: One, the central coast, beach dunes, marshes, river valleys, oak and pine mountains; two, the Central Valley, wide, shallow lakes, swamps, valley oaks along the streams; three, the Sierra Nevada, chaparral to tundra to mixed-conifer forests; four, the Modoc Plateau, sagebrush, juniper, volcano country; five, the Klamath Coast, mountains up to Trinidad Head; finally, the coast valleys and mountains south of the Tehachapis, with a huge population drawing water from the Colorado, the Owens and Great Central Valleys.

INTERVIEWER: You're not including the Mojave. And how about the White Mountains?

JP: That's not core California. They belong to the Great Basin or the lower Colorado. We're summery, Mediterranean. Our smell is out of oily, aromatic herbs and olive-green shrubs, grass, and dark forest.

From Terry Kalisch, "Interview with Joe Pittman,"
La Puerta 6, no. 3 (summer 1995)

THE KENERETS

[1]

Marcia could tell by the hats. Ez had a hundred of them. One of the first things he did when they went anywhere was buy a hat. Years ago, trying— and failing—to get permission to do location work in Moscow and Leningrad, he'd consoled himself by buying fur towers at the dollar store in the hotel. In Africa, he bought white-hunter crush hats. From Bora Bora and Fiji, he brought back sun hats with mesh and cloth panels. He had Sherpa hats, fox skin on one side, fox fur on the other. He had fedoras from his father with the initials ɪJK in gold on an inside band. There were varieties of tennis and quasi-military hats. When the dictation started, he wore—for authority, for confidence—a gold-braided commodore's hat.

He and Hypatia had begun working in the study but then shifted to the fieldstone table which he'd ordered twenty years ago for the terrace after he'd seen the one from which Karen Blixen—one of Marcia's favorite writers—dispensed medicine and wisdom to her black neighbors in the Ngong hills. What had been for Blixen a convenience, maybe a necessity before World War I—when the availability and transport of furniture from Copenhagen was a matter of months and risk—was here, like so much else in Southern California, out of place. Or not out of place, because that would have suggested that some particular style belonged here. One of the things the young Marcia had hated—and in which she now delighted—was that there was almost no object or style which couldn't be an integral part of Southern California. Oddly, Marcia was more conscious of this than people who'd moved here even twenty or thirty years ago.

She'd grown up not in these expensive West L.A. precincts but in the Valley. In the fifties, her father, a film cutter at RKO, had bought a house in Encino a mile west of what became the San Diego Freeway, three blocks south of the Ventura. (Had he lived into the eighties, the sale of their small house would have eased the old age he never reached.)

College had given Marcia the distance she'd craved. College itself wasn't distant—she'd gone downcoast to San Diego State—but what she learned there was. For years, she and her mother had talked of her going east to college, but her mother died and her father dangled over a financial pit, and there was no way to swing it. All through Encino High, the thought of going to an eastern college had insulated her from the gaudy stupidity and crassness she felt around her in schools and malls. Two more years, one more year, six months, three months, one month, and then there was no scholarship for her at Smith, Barnard, or Mount Holyoke. Her father held her hands and said, "I can't swing it, baby. The studio's bleeding. I could get laid off any month. If there weren't good schools out here, I'd risk a second mortgage. But there are." She said it didn't matter, but it did. California seemed like prison. She disliked the almost-seasonless weather, the houses, the freeways, the palms, the cancerous sunlight. She hated film talk and most movies.

At San Diego State, everything changed. There were the same sunlight, the same palms, some of the same kids, but there were also Dr. Shojai and Professor Neill, who opened doors through which Marcia Glasser floated.

When she met Ez, she was halfway reconciled to films. (*The Last Tycoon*—the book, not the movie—showed her there could be greatness out here.) Still, after college, she meant to go east, as far as possible—New York, Paris, Rome, Vienna—but her father was pensioned off in her junior year and died two months before her graduation, leaving nothing but the mortgaged house. Marcia went to work for a production company as a reader. Her boss, Myron Blumenthal, told her she had a gift for spotting material, though in three years with him, not a single property which she recommended went beyond first option. Still, she was in the swim of it. She read the trades, devoured—and spread—gossip, fattened her Rolodex, and became a significant speck.

One day in Armando's, Myron introduced her to Ez. For a film person, it was like meeting Lincoln, or, at least—Ez corrected her when she told him—Chester A. Arthur. She'd been living with Larry Dienstack, the youngest broker in the Dean Witter office on Wilshire, a wisecracking, nervous kid, who, she'd begun noticing, was looking for something flashier than a girl who wore no makeup, didn't like the beach, subscribed to literary magazines, and saw at least five films a week.

A month later, she was working for Ez, first as a location scout, then a shooting scheduler. He was making *Wilda Has Moved,* and she was sent to Mexico to scout locations. When he came down too—it was to Zihuatanejo—they stayed in one of Floyd Harmel's houses and began their love life. It pushed his shaky marriage to Elizabeth over the cliff. A week before *Wilda's* screening in Long Beach, they married.

Most of her adult life had been spent with Ez, and life without him was unimaginable. The terror of losing him was an element of its sweetness. Despite his vitality, Ezra and Marcia faced the numbers: Ez sixty-two, sixty-three, sixty-four; Marcia forty, forty-one, forty-two.

[2]

A week after Keneret, weak as a rag, returned from the hernia surgery—his stomach had slipped through the hernia into his chest—he opened a letter from Agnes Desoger.

I am writing in the hope that I may persuade you to participate in our INTERNATIONAL FILMMAKERS BIOGRAPHY SERIES, a reference project that publishes autobiographies and biographies of the world's leading filmmakers. We note that there is no full-length biography of you, and only two full-length studies of your films, including the recent one by Wendell Spear. Our hope is that you would consent to write, or to dictate to an assistant (whom we could supply), an essay of ten thousand words or more about your life and work.

"Why the 'we' and 'our'?" he grumbled. Agnes was no stranger. For that matter, HAL, Inc., wouldn't exist if he hadn't plucked Leet out of the middle of the Pacific. The personal insult of the impersonal: "Like the reverse insult, strangers using your first name."

The rest of the letter concerned the fee—three thousand dollars—the distribution, largely to libraries, and a list of "your peers already included in the series." Agnes added that she was sending "under separate cover" the W volume, with essays "by or on" Walsh, Wanger, Welles, Wellman, Wenders, Wilder, Wise, and Wyler.

Lying in bed by his untouched breakfast tray, Keneret said, "She asks me to write about myself when there's no self left."

Marcia: "That's the postoperative self talking."

Keneret: "The post-Duggan-dumped self."

[3]

He was waking at three in the morning after forced walks around his room, then the house, the garden, the block. He tried reading, not the pile of scripts—they were a memento mori—but new books. Here, too, though, there was trouble: he read as he'd been reading for forty years, visualizing, dramatizing, filming. He'd have to learn how to read a story for its own sake. Nights, in their Super Imperial bed, he dreamily foraged for hope, strength, a way to come back. By seven o'clock, still the household breakfast time, he and Marcia were often exhausted. He tried to concentrate on the paper, to relish his mango juice, muesli, muffin, and coffee, the fragrance of the garden, but though his body strengthened, his mind didn't. Once he said, as if reading it in the paper, "Keneret's occupation's gone."

"Take your walk, darling."

"That's not an occupation." He put on a wide-billed sun hat and took off down Ninth Street. His octogenarian neighbor, Mrs. Iwinaga, was adding a plastic rose to her ritual bush. "How you fearing today?

"Okay, Mrs. Iwinaga. How's mister today?"

"He eat egg, getting bettah." The ninety-four-year-old toothless smiler sat on the little porch in his Dodgers cap; he took it off and waved at Keneret. He too had recently returned from surgery, the latest of almost-annual operations. "I take him quick from hospital. People die there. How your scar?"

He knew she wanted to look at the fourteen-inch scimitar on his back and side. She tried for an exchange, lifting her sweater to exhibit her own, an ancient riverbed running south in a network of body seams, inches too close to Mr. Iwinaga's old playground for Keneret's comfort. "Behaving itself," he said.

Home, he came quietly up to Marcia adrift on the terrace. The sun had lit what he hadn't noticed till now, streaks of silver in her brown hair. He also noticed the depth of lines in her forehead and around her mouth. His beloved wife was aging. That was fine, was right, but looking at her from the side as she dreamed off skyward, Keneret suddenly felt that he was age's agent: his postoperative, postdumped gloom was pushing and deepening the process.

He made a little noise, startling her. "Excuse me, sweetheart. Should have called. I had a good walk, feel better." He told her of the exchange with Mrs. Iwinaga.

"She'll outlast me, and you can marry her."

"What I've been hoping for years."

She said, "I've been thinking."

"Yes?"

"I think that you should think about Agnes's invitation."

"Remind me."

"Just after you came home from Cedars. Your autobiography. Some encyclopedia or Who's Who thing. You know, she sent that book with family pictures of the directors and their biographies."

"Right. Willie Wyler, Orson. I looked at a couple of them. Pretty interesting. Not for me, though. I don't write. If you want it, you write it."

"The point is for you to do it. Any way you want, dates and facts, impressions, memories. I'm sure they'd fix it up, if that's what worries you."

"It doesn't worry me. I just don't give a goddamn about it. Looking back's no substitute for doing something."

Marcia was no nag, but it was clear that this was something she was serious about. Maybe she wanted something more of him in case something happened, a substitute for the children they didn't have. Yet she didn't know what it would mean to do it, especially now, as he was falling down the arc of his career.

She said, "Writing's doing something. You've seen plenty, you've known plenty, you've done plenty."

"Like most old gents."

"Not like most. Nobody in the world knows what you know. Nobody thinks like you."

"That's just one of my troubles."

"Don't deprecate yourself out of this, please. Think about it. Please, Ez."

[4]

That morning, he went into his study—shelves of film books, scripts, the desk he wrote letters on—and sat, pen poised over a pad of yellow paper. "Hell," he said, then wrote, *I was born in August 1930, nine months after the market crashed! My father, a cotton-goods salesman, was forty-one. My mother. . . .* And stopped. The opacity of the words, their inability to expose the actuality behind them—no, not for him. His father, Ira James Keneret, IJ, the flat, black-fringed head, the clear autumn-colored eyes, the innocent eyes of a blindly innocent man. My number-1 booster. How to put him—let alone their relationship—into sentences? He'd spent five or six thousand days living with Ira J. and Mildred Keneret. Thousands and thousands of words-looks-touches among them. How to make sense of what that meant? A camera could have shown IJ's gray suits and blue ties, his head bent into a tent of the *New York Times*, right hand curled around a coffee cup, the mild voice—was it tenor or baritone?—the razored cheek Ezra kissed till the day, twenty years ago, the nonagenarian IJ coughed and died.

Sentences didn't do it. At least, not his.

Making a film was social. You were on the phone; you had meetings with writers, producers, actors, designers, unit directors. It was your film, but you talked as much as thought it out. Even when you did the writing, you couldn't guess how others would film it, act it, how it would look. You weren't alone, as a colony creature is never alone.

"Writing's for hermits," he told Marcia. "I wasn't made for it. I've gotta talk things out with people."

"Agnes suggested you dictate to somebody, like Wendell did to Leet. Maybe you could use her."

"She's a big exec now."

"All right. Give Agnes a call, or Wendell, or Billy Wilder. Ask him how he did it."

"He was a writer. I'm not, and I can't talk to a machine. I can't do memos that way."

"You've dictated letters to a secretary."

"I don't have a secretary anymore. I don't have a base."

"Call a casting director. Call Reuben, he'll find you anything you want."

"I'm not looking for an actress."

"Actresses are looking for work. Between jobs, they'd love taking dictation from a great director."

"Does Liz Taylor know shorthand?"

"Okay, dictate to me. No, I won't do. You'd be inhibited. You've got to forget everything but what you feel about what you remember."

"I can't talk to someone who doesn't know what words mean, what a comma is. Anyway, if she's an actress, she'll take off for the first part that's dangled in front of her."

"Put an ad in the paper. Call a secretarial agency. This is not a genuine difficulty."

"The point is," he said, "it is."

But he called Agnes, who sent over Hypatia.

[5]

Wearing a white-and-blue commodore's cap, Keneret walked up and down the terrace in front of the stone table on which Hypatia kept her laptop, purse, and a glass of ice water which she refilled from a spigot in the wall fridge. In the purse was a little Olympia camera which, after asking his permission, she used every now and then between dictation sessions to snap his picture. "Your look changes with what you dictate."

Keneret had been behind cameras too many years to question photographers' motives. What the hell, let the girl do something she cared about. "So it shouldn't be a total loss," he told Marcia.

"She's getting more out of this than you'd believe."

"I bore her to death."

"Right. You're the death of everyone. I hope she'll give us some of the pictures."

"Glutton." Kissing the forehead. The silver hair was gone. How long had this been going on? All these years, Marcia couldn't wait to catch up to his age. Now, when it approached, out came the dye. Another jolt of pity. Free-falling from his professional life, he was still, while he had her, more or less of a piece.

[6]

Keneret chopped and shaped the air to help him shape the verbal re-creation of his life. Sometimes it went like jazz, and Hypatia, using her shorthand of squiggles, numbers, letters, dashes, and words, shrieked, "Too fast." Her head and body usually swayed to the rhythm of dictation.

He thought her a strange person, too passionate to take dictation, but she was also deferential. Was that a shard of Central Europe's feudal courtesy? Her thin face was rich with reaction, every inch of it tense with the words she stroked. Bone thin, her cheekbones and nose made an M, the green eyes O's. The right eye was smaller, though almost an A. *Amo,* her face read. But what did she love? Clearly not meat and potatoes. She had no hips, only bones suspending her yellow slacks; no belly, just a place for a belly. Breasts she had, and was free with them.

Fine, thought Marcia. Anything that helps him.

One thing Hypatia did love, it turned out, was film. After following Oscar Harmel from Kenya to Hollywood, she studied cinematography at UCLA. She told Keneret that since she was a girl in Zagreb, she'd been reading books about movies.

In their first days together, Keneret, trying not to sink into the word-ocean, spent more time gabbing about movies than dictating to her. "It's easier than self-excavation," he told Marcia, who, he mistakenly thought, was disappointed in how little he'd done.

"That's why you have a girl, not a Dictaphone."

"I don't believe my life's worth telling. It's boring. It wasn't—isn't—boring to live, but I'd never buy it for a film."

"The outside maybe, not the inside. Tell what you're thinking, even about me. I don't care what you say."

"Yeah? Wait'll I unload."

"I have a little load too." She was in back of him now, hands kneading his shoulders and neck, the tension there as familiar to her as the lawn. "Talk about the films, how you made them, what they're about."

"Never. That's not my job. I only had"—the preterit brought him up short—"to make them."

[7]

Hypatia was a fan of *Lianne Takes Jimmy.*

"People call it my thirties comedy."

The *Amo* opened to plain O. "Really!"

"Really." He took off. "I didn't like those pictures. Maybe a few of Hawks's and Wyler's. Ford, of course—*Lianne* wouldn't exist without *The Informer* and *My Darling Clementine*—but most of them . . . infantile. I laughed at them when I was ten. And *Casablanca!* Claptrap. That wind-in-the-hair flashback with the Arch of Triumph, those characters out of the Warner Brothers bin. But when I was a kid, I saw *Citizen Kane* at the RKO Eighty-first Street on a Saturday and went back Sunday—first time I'd seen a movie twice, let alone on successive days—and that was it. I didn't know what a cubist was, had never heard of Joyce—I may have heard the name Stravinsky on WQXR—but after *Citizen Kane*, I became a modern. And I wanted to make films."

[8]

The preparation for what should have been simple, walking into his study—they kept shifting venues—started when he woke in the morning.

There was the drip of dawn, then the light overtaking the honeysuckle, the bougainvillea, the magnolias, the palms which screened his bedroom from Ocean Drive and the Pacific. "Does the world need more Keneret today?" He shifted to another pillow, flexed his toes to generate circulation, felt Marcia's bare legs, the debris of desire. Up, more obligations: knee bends, pull-and-sit-ups

Six-twenty, four hours before Hypatia showed up with her Wang. Where had they stopped? Oh yes, Miss Truxell telling the class, "It's 1936 now. Write '1936' at the top of the paper." Six years old; FDR president, bad Hitler over there squeezing Kenerets, though not yet to death. Edward VIII abdicated. He and Momma listened to him on the radio. The king's voice was slow, the words beautiful. Did that lead him to English girls, English actresses? Maybe it was why his closest friend was an Englishman.

Brushing his teeth—there were twenty-five toothbrushes aligned like long parti-colored teeth in porcelain holders around the washbasin—slipping into loafers, putting on his commodore's cap. Ezra Keneret's life waiting like a series of zeros for the digit which would make it count. Suddenly, fury: that monster Duggan and his stinking handyman, Vlach the Destroyer, had robbed him of this digit, had condemned him to scooping this verbal muck out of his head.

Down on the carpet, left knee to his chest, then right, fifteen times. Twenty minutes later, he walked past the Iwinagas, head full not of 1936, Momma, Poppa, Grandpa, and Eileen, but fury—Duggan, Vlach, the *Times*, Spielberg, Lucas, Di Palma, Paramount, the weasels who didn't know or care how important it was that Ezra Keneret should go on making films.

The IPO outdid the Kleiner Perkins expectations. NET-SCRAWL opened at 14, hit 31 by 10:30, 64 by noon, 71 by 2:00, and settled at 59 by closing.

Three years earlier, Buddy Tyndall was living on peanut butter in a trailer south of Lincoln, Nebraska. On Tuesday night, he was worth four billion dollars.

Tyndall flies his Gulfstream X450 back to San José from France (where he owns a house in the Bois de Boulogne). His Arabian filly, Saana, has done herself proud at Long-champs. In San José, he changes to one of his five Line-topper helicopters and flies to the pad over the stables where he checks on Mrs. Chips, his three-year-old Preak-ness-bound mare, then is chauffeured in one of his four Bentleys to the house where Doreen is just back from re-doing their Sutton Place triplex. Over dinner on the ter-race, he says, "What's happenin', Dor? We're supposed to be sittin' in the catbird seat?"

Doreen's hands work their glittery way through her black hair. "We're in it, Bud. It's just that we been using it as a latrine."

From A. M. Storcher,
The Siliconnaires (Viking, 1998)

SPEARS AND ABARBANELS

[1]

At Grinnell, to Spear's surprise, Amelia had become politically and socially conservative to a degree which led to jocular, then unjocular, arguments. Her support of Richard Nixon particularly angered him even as he knew that its source was less admiration for the twisted president than his anger. His sometimes stuttered rebuttals, ironic and fierce, brought her what she wanted, his shame that he'd overpowered the loving daughter who was doing little more than staking out her independence.

Amelia was upset about the move to the Malibu hills cabin, yet tried to help her mother adjust to it. When Vanessa died, Amelia's mourning took the form of preparing him to be alone. (It didn't take much; he'd felt alone for years.) Two years later, when there was a chance that he would marry Bebe Rosch, she was so enthusiastic that it reinforced his sense that solitude was his destiny. Bebe, like Vanessa, did not want to live isolated in a Malibu canyon.

Amelia married James Abarbanel, a lanky, intelligent jokester with whom Spear got on perfectly. James had turned away from his father's world and worked in St. Louis, first for Washington University as a programmer, then for Anheuser Busch as salesman and sales manager. Amelia worked there until Jennifer arrived, then became what she still was, a full-time housewife, parent, and unpaid volunteer for school and civic projects.

Spear's biannual visits to St. Louis and the Abarbanels' almost-annual ones to Malibu—he paid for their motel rooms on the Coast Highway—were for him happy ones, although their domestic sloppiness first astonished, then upset, him. After an hour's visit, his cabin looked as if it had been pillaged, and the mess of their large house was, as he saw it, a health hazard. He said little but wondered much what this domestic chaos meant. (In retrospect, it pointed to the inner contradictions which led Amelia to put up the wall between them.)

When Jennifer was ten, Amelia became an exercise and diet freak. "Freak" because she crossed some psychic line and became gaunt, almost skeletal. On one visit, Spear was so shocked by her appearance that he asked what her doctor said about it. She said, "I'm an exceptionally healthy person," then added, strangely, "I wish you were."

For years, food had been Amelia's bugbear. After reading Simone de Beauvoir on a woman's contingent and cyclical role—replacing and filling—she'd resolved that her identity was never going to be submerged by the preparation and service of food. She did cook but so tastelessly it became a family joke at which no one laughed louder than she. In St. Louis, James did a lot of the cooking, and there were many takeouts.

Amelia's house too was on a sort of diet. She began replacing what were once comfortable sofas and chairs with spindle-legged fragilities on which people were rightly afraid to sit. When he offered to buy a few of the old, comfortable sort, she said, "What we have is perfect for us." Each year also saw fewer decorations, whatnots, and pictures in the house. One year, Spear shipped her a lovely pseudo-Fragonard painting he'd found in the back of a La Cienega gallery. It was full of round, pink-cheeked people cavorting in an elegant drawing room. Everybody expressed delight in it, but when he next visited, it was nowhere to be seen. When he asked Amelia about it, she said, "I gave it to Grandpa Abarbanel. It belongs to his mental era—and yours." On his last visit, the Abarbanel walls were bare except for a—to Spear—defiantly ugly Dubuffet reproduction and five or six of Jennifer's primary-school daubs.

Amelia wore shapeless sacks to conceal her body. Spear knew that she sensed and resented what she regarded as chauvinist disgust with her appearance. Bravado masked her confusion and fear. Her voice, which had been exceptionally lovely, was often sharp with metallic falsity. It meant that she was hiding what she felt; yet, more and more, the feelings and the opinions they generated were a problem for him, less in themselves than in their intensity and belligerence. No one but James and Jennifer challenged her, and it became impossible to joke with her about the contents of her widening net of contempt.

More than anything, she hated California and what she called "your business." Growing up, she hadn't wanted to leave; her ambition was to go to Berkeley or Stanford. He and Vanessa had to persuade her that it might be good to see the rest of the country. At Grinnell, she even practiced his trade and wrote movie reviews, quite good ones, for the school paper. Now she wouldn't go to movies, and when others talked about them, she turned away or said something like "Can't we find something serious to talk about?"

Spear didn't know if this was a repudiation of him or a form of self-abandonment, the burial of her ambition and talent. Marcia Keneret told him that she had once felt the same way and that he shouldn't worry about it, it was a phase. "It just started later for Amelia than it did for me."

"I think the late start means deeper rootage," said Spear. "I see no signs of its passing."

After a while, there were no more visits to California, and things began to go wrong with his visits to St. Louis: "We're going away" or "We have visitors using the guest room." He'd visited them every Christmas for fifteen years. That stopped. As did her letters. She'd been a wonderful letter writer, and he'd saved all her letters. She knew this, and he knew that that was one reason she no longer wrote him. She was consciously depriving him of pleasure. Why? This he didn't know, and then didn't want to know.

Her telephone calls got briefer and rarer. After a while, the only time she called was on his birthday, and then she sang a self-mocking "Happy Birthday," asked a few perfunctory questions, and said she had to go somewhere. When he phoned, she was always in a great hurry; she had to pick something up or someone was there with her. If he tried to talk about something personal, she'd say, "You have it all wrong, Dad," or even "You never get things right."

When Jennifer graduated from law school, Amelia did come out to California with James. They assembled in Davis, and he'd taken them to dinner. Amelia had looked preoccupied. She'd been preparing to say what she did when she and James took off for the airport: "I don't think it would be a good idea for you to see Jennifer when she starts work in San Francisco. I don't think she should be distracted. In fact, Dad, I think for a while, you and I should keep some distance between us." While his mouth hung open and his heart broke in his chest, she got into the taxi next to James, who smiled and waved good-bye. It was a terrible moment which, for a while, he thought he might not survive.

[2]

Both Spear and Jennifer spent her third California Christmas alone. He didn't want to impose on her; and she didn't want to suggest that she needed him. Each pretended to be going somewhere for Christmas dinner, Spear to Cousin Hugh's, Jennifer to the Morgans'. Christmas morning, he telephoned.

"Thank you so much for the wine, Grandpa. I think it's the first case I've ever had. You shouldn't have—not after that wonderful check."

"My pleasure, darling, and thank you for the beautiful argyles. I didn't think anybody under fifty knew how to knit anymore."

"Mom taught me when I was eight. I enjoy it, it calms me. I just didn't have time for a while. I'm making you another pair now."

As he said, "That's more than I'm entitled to," he felt the chill of that extra time. "I'm going to put these on and wear them through Christmas. It'll almost be like having you here."

"I miss you too, Grandpa. If I hadn't promised Shari, I think I'd just fly down. But it's probably better for me. I don't suppose you've spoken to Mom."

"No change there."

"It'll change someday, I know it will."

"Perhaps it will."

"She called me at seven forty-five; I don't think I sounded too good."

"You did to her. You do to me. Merry Christmas, darling."

It was a strange day for Spear. He hadn't been alone on Christmas since—he hardly remembered 1949 in Florence, the week after breaking up with the French art student Marie France de Fauconnier, who'd come to him on the rebound from a Norman aristocrat whose family had found hers untouchable. He'd thought she was an aristocrat. Reading Proust that lonely Christmas opened the complexity of feudal aristocracy to him. He relished it in Proust as he hated its English reality. Everything in Proust enchanted him and it was a wonderful Christmas. The volumes got him through loneliness and the Florentine chill. (The floor in his room at the Villa Fabricotti was marble; the cold knifed through two pairs of wool socks and froze his fingers as he turned the pages.)

Now he had the loneliness but not the Proust, and instead of love-despair and youth, he had scotch, age, and fear.

Christmas and Boxing Day passed, then Twelfth Night and the holiday birthdays of King, Lincoln, and Washington. Spear did his taxes, gardened, walked, watched films on the VCR, wrote them up in his journal, looked at birds, the sky, the flowers. March, April, May, June. A year since Fer had lost her job, and there was still no job.

Spear found it awkward to speak about it with her. Jennifer did tell him about interviews "coming up next week" or "when he gets back from New York." Only occasionally did she sound anxious: "Sometimes I wonder if there's anything out there for me." Spear's stomach looped in fear. Should he say something to her about cutting expenses, moving in with a friend? How else could she cut down? She had to eat, to look decent. She couldn't be without a car, not in California. "Fer, have you thought about temp work?"

"I thought I told you, Grandpa. I took a contingency case in March. Spent forty or fifty hours on it—and lost. Can't do that again."

"You didn't tell me, no. I was wondering about public defenders. I know they don't get paid as well as you used to, but aren't they needed? Something you could do till something better turns up?"

"I've had my application in for months. They have their pick of lawyers, and not just ex-associates."

What to do? Pretty soon he'd have to talk with her father about working something out. They could transfer some equities to her. He'd pull in his belt, drink cheaper whiskey, cut down on the cigars, cancel subscriptions. He certainly wouldn't buy the Sickert drawing he'd been eyeing in the Sotheby catalog.

Still, all this wouldn't do it. Stopgaps were stopgaps; but the gap widening with no closure in sight was in him. He began to have headaches, stomachaches.

"You better cut down on the scotch and cigars," said Keneret.

"I have. I do."

"When's the last time you had a checkup?"

"No idea. I don't need one. This business with Jennifer is dragging on me. I've got to find her something."

"No you don't. She'll find something herself, when she's good and ready. What you need is to get away. It'll be good for her and good for you." Large and authoritative, Keneret banged his right hand on his left palm for emphasis.

"Get away where? Why?"

"Doesn't matter where. Maybe St. Louis. Make up with Amelia. It would make everybody happy."

"We're like the Middle East. You going to be our Kissinger?"

"All right. Go see old haunts, Oxford, Paris, Florence. Go birding on the moors."

"Sure. I'm up to sixty kilometers on a bicycle."

"What about that think tank on Lake Como that invited you?"

"What a memory. Can you see me chattering about Dante and Murnau with German physicists and Bombay sociologists?"

"You bet I can. I wish they'd invited me. The point is to go somewhere, anywhere that gets you out of Jennifer's hair and her troubles out of what's left of yours. Come down to Santa Monica with us. Marcia would love it."

"Sure she would. Everyone loves *The Man Who Came to Dinner.*" He searched for matches but, remembering, put the unlit cigar in his mouth. "I wish to God I could smoke this. Why should I give up what I love?" He spread his arms, an air hug for his cabin.

"Did I tell you Ira Stein said he might be able to find a place for her in his office?"

"I told her. She doesn't want to work down here."

"I don't blame her. Mudslides, riots. Now these damn fires. Took me nearly forty minutes to get up here today. The point is that there are places for her when she's ready."

"Actually, she tries to tell me that too. But it's nearly a year and a half. It's frightening."

"I swear to you, Wendell. If worse comes to worst, I can use her myself, and I don't mean another Hypatia. I'll ask Ira to assign her to my affairs and yours and three or four other people's. She'll more than earn her keep."

Spear lit his cigar, went to the bottle of Chivas Regal, and poured himself a glassful. "Scotch?" he called out to Keneret, but his friend was up.

"I better get going. I don't want to get stuck. I hope you won't have any trouble up here."

[3]

While he cooked his hamburger, Spear sipped whiskey and, watching the fires on the television news, sipped more. He must have been alert enough to turn off the set, because when he woke to shouts and banging on his door, the set was dark. Dazed, he made out his name: "Spear, Mr. Spear!" His door chimes were ringing. There was more banging. "You gotta get out. Fire! You gotta get out now."

Spear hustled to the door, opened it on two wild-eyed young men, one of whom was Roger Kobble. "What? What. . . ."

"Mr. Spear," said Roger, "you've got to hurry. Right now. Get your car and drive down to the station or the Coast Motel. We gotta warn others. Take care," and they drove off in the station truck.

Spear ran for his car keys, his wallet, and, on the way out, grabbed the bottle of scotch. He set off down the road in his Mustang. It was very dark, strangely calm, though from uphill, he heard something like a sucking sound, as if the hill were sighing. His head was clear now, and he drove carefully around the curves, down to the ocean. Soon he was part of a long queue of cars, almost unheard of up here. The Pacific Highway was a parking lot, and a casting call, people in nightgowns, raincoats, furs, sweaters, slacks. Several people were in evening dress. There were lots of children in pajamas. Many were being held. Many couples held each other. Police whirl lights lit faces, which looked stunned, drained, scared, furious. A fire truck escorted by a marshal's car made its way up the hill. Spear watched the red light disappear, then saw, far away, a flame knife out of the blackness. There were screams from others who'd seen it. Then a smaller flame, gold and blue, broke out in another part of the dark. Heart pumping fast, head like a struck gong, Spear got back in his car and opened the scotch. He was shivering. Some old knowledge stirred in his bones. What was it? Yes, the war, Grandpa Wallace holding his hand, walking near the Thames. A plane, a gray ghost, was overhead, then a whine and a shower of light. A six-story building down the block shook like a huge plum pudding, then fell on itself; there was smoke, fire, a storm of glass, brick dust, people running. He was running with Grandpa, heart beating so fast he felt it would leap from his chest.

"Oh, God," he said now. "The cabin. My cabin."

[4]

At six, in what his watch said was A.M.—the air was dark with ash—he started the car and drove toward his road. A police car blocked it; a policeman said, "You can't go up there."

"I don't see any fire."

"They think they've put it out, but it's still dangerous. Only firemen can go up."

"I live up there."

"You'd better find a place to stay tonight."

Spear turned the car around and drove south on 101. The Coast Motel had the NO VACANCY sign out; so did the next motel and the three after that. Spear found a phone booth, but the phone didn't function. He drove to Santa Monica.

Marcia opened the door. "Oh, thank God. Your phone's been out. We were terrified for you." She embraced him. Ez came out in pajamas and, for the first time in his life, embraced him also.

After he washed up and put on—folded up—a pair of Ez's slacks and tied on his bathrobe, he joined them on the terrace. Over coffee and eggs served by the beautiful Filipino cook, Lourdes, he told them what had happened, then called an enormously relieved Jennifer.

"I'll call Mom. I know she's been worried sick about you." That was the best note in the hours since he'd left the cabin.

[5]

Two days later, he drove back up the half-melted road, which had been cleared of charred branches and ash. There were piles of them on what had been asphalt shoulders. Ash particles floated in the air, which was foul, death heavy, the smell of bombed London. After a mile, the road was as strange to him as if he'd never lived here. When he came on a neighbor's house intact, his heart raced with hope. Beyond, though, there was little but ash, rubble, charred branches, stripped and broken trees. He drove past what had been his driveway, then, after half a mile, turned back and recognized it. He parked on the road and walked through smoking rubble to the black stumps which had been his cabin. He picked up a long-handled aluminum skimmer from a pile of shards and, pushing it through more piles, found pots, a framed picture, a toilet bowl, a sink, even, surprisingly, a few books, one of which, a precious eighteenth-century folio, was, amazingly, just slightly blackened. It was the only important survivor. Walking carefully, shaking his head, Spear groaned and talked aloud. "It's over, over, over." On what had been the terrace, he picked up, then dropped, what looked like a piece of black jade: a scorched squirrel. "I can't, can't." There was a scraping noise, frightening. Spear looked around. Twenty yards away, he saw a deer foraging on a black twist of branch. For some reason, Spear picked up and tossed it the squirrel. The deer's wild eyes were dark—as Spear saw them—with their common ruin.

[6]

That he should be here in St. Louis, sleeping in his granddaughter's old room, looking at the looping strands of a willow tree as she'd looked at them the first twenty years of her life, was still, in his third week here, as strange to him as the metamorphosis of his angry daughter into the loving daughter she had once been.

Perhaps it was his metamorphosis that had brought hers about: from an authoritative, householding husband, father, lecturer, and critic, to a homeless, jobless, wifeless old man. Amelia had taken in this reduced self and become its thoughtful, affectionate, amusing caretaker and companion. He was her concern, her occupation. There was no alien metal in her voice. They walked, shopped, went to the zoo, the aviary, attended lectures at Washington University, concerts, and the opera. Almost every day they lunched in a different restaurant. The internal devil that had shoved her toward disappearance had itself disappeared. She ate with appetite and ease, hungrily, even greedily, pasta, pizza, burgers, melts. What he left on his plate, she took on hers. They drank wine. He smoked cigars, and they talked about everything, Jennifer, Vanessa, James, Grandpa Abarbanel, his father's rectory, England, Florence. Who would have guessed that the ruination of his life would have led to this?

"You can live here always, Dad."

James too, solid, amused, busy not only marketing beer but with volunteer work for the schools, bicycle paths, and Mississippi River reclamation projects, also seemed to enjoy his father-in-law's presence. "It's wonderful for Amelia," he told Spear.

Then the temperature sank, snow fell, and Spear knew he wasn't going to spend much more time as a pensioner in his daughter's house. He remembered his father's pastoral calls to shriveling elders tilted into shafts of sun, chins resting on the knobs of canes, dwindling toward the cemetery. Maybe it was not the worst way to slide off the earth, but it was not his way.

In his sixth and penultimate St. Louis week, Spear received a check from the home insurance company for almost twice as much as he'd expected. It was clear that he could rebuild the cabin, but in one of those life-deciding half seconds, he knew he wouldn't. Ten days earlier, he'd had a call from the Astrid Templeton Foundation renewing an offer made and remade over the last years to buy his property for the wildlife preserve it wanted to set up in the Malibu hills. Instead of taking advantage of his fire-ruined property, they'd unaccountably doubled their highest offer. Spear telephoned Zack Wool and asked him to assess his tax situation. Wool called back the next day and told him that he'd be in very good shape.

"All monied up and no place to go," said Spear.

"You know Realtors out here."

"Why out there?"

"I see. Well, in St. Louis, then, if that suits you better. I can understand that. The fire, your daughter."

"No, it's not that, Zack. For some reason, I think the world lies all before me. This world and the next."

"I don't like the sound of that, Wendell. I don't want to lose a client."

"You won't lose this one. I've had my fill of loss."

The most unexpected consequence of the fire had to do with Jennifer. Ira Stein, Keneret's lawyer, called Keneret who called Spear who called Jennifer to tell her that Pacific Shoreline Mortgage Insurers was immediately hiring lawyers to deal with the legal problems raised by the Southern California fires. "I know you weren't keen about working in the L.A. area, darling, but Ira thinks this is a terrific opportunity. Refinancing, subordinated mortgage securities, construction loans, I forget what else."

"I know something about property law, Grandpa. At SB and C, I did some work for a real-estate investment trust. Will you thank Mr. Stein for me? I'll get in touch with them today."

[7]

A week later, Jennifer called her parents and grandfather to tell them that she was on staff with PSMI. The salary was sixteen thousand dollars more than she'd made her third year at SB&C. "And I like the people enormously."

Especially, it turned out, one person, the man who'd interviewed her, the supervising partner, Jay Volkman, "a thirty-eight-year-old divorcé," as Spear learned in the first call he made to Jennifer from the beautiful villa of the Sproul Foundation in the hills above Lake Como.

*　　*　　*　　*

JP: We're part of the Pacific Rim system. Our un- and dis-
employment, our immigrants, our maquiladorization, our
Crips and Bloods, our high-school macho zombies, aren't
isolated phenomena. They're inextricably involved with the
vaporization of two trillion dollars of fictional capital on
the Tokyo stock exchange; with the robotization of the two
Koreas, the seesawing of the two Chinas. Our underclasses
are brothers of the Ainus, the aborigines and islanders
whose life span is less than half of our middle class's. Connected like the winds and currents of the Pacific: El Niño
and La Niña don't stay in their backyard. Doom here is
doom there.

INTERVIEWER: I don't know whether you're more like Jeremiah or Karl Marx.

JP: Jeremiah? No. Marx, maybe. I'm not here to moan and
complain. I want to change things. Marx knew how the human body figured in labor, value, and exchange. You don't
get that from Uncle Miltie Friedman. Money supply isn't
in Genesis and it won't be in Revelations.

From Terry Kalisch, "Interview with Joe Pittman,"
La Puerta 6, no. 3 (summer 1995)

SPEAR ★ Abroad and Home

[1]

Melanie Minolitte had been drawn to Lake Como by *La Chartreuse de Parme*. Its hero, Fabrizio del Dongo, was born in Griante—Stendhal misspelled it Granta—and its wonderful heroine, the Countess Gina Sanseverina, grew up among the hills, which, she boasted, "were never forced to yield a return." Everything there was "noble and speaks of love." The chestnuts and wild cherry trees still colored the slopes, and, beyond them, Melanie could see the Alps. There was a history of the villa in her room, a train of names and dates to those who'd never lived here, but for Melanie a delight. The famous villa of Pliny the Elder might have been on this very promontory; Augustus Caesar had been the region's proconsul; Bonaparte made Josephine's son Eugene its viceroy; the *luminati*, Beccaria, Verri, and the Abbé Parini, lived in this and other villas up and down the lake-hugging hills; just across the lake, Benito Mussolini had been shot by a *partigiano* colonel before being strung upside down in a Milanese piazzetta next to his mistress, Claretta Petacci; John F. Kennedy, days from proclaiming in Berlin that he was a jelly doughnut ("*Ich bin ein Berliner*"), took over the villa for a night with some world-class Sophia or Gina (diplomatic mist veiled the identity).

The randy president closed out the official history, but scholars, scientists, artists, industrialists, and officials from every country, researching and conferencing in the villa's studies and salons, made and were making a different sort. One of them, Melanie's own Hansl, spent ten hours a day merged a little more intensely than she liked with his computer, much of his passion spent in outbreaks of fury at its dark seizures. Meanwhile, she read in the handsome library and looked across the lake at the stone brows of Mount Grigna, following the white ferryboats which, every quarter of an hour, stitched their wakes from Bellagio to Como, Menaggio to Varenna, Cadenabbia to Lecco. Reading, looking, dreaming, she waited for lunch, the gathering of the Fellows (a quarter of them women) around the risotti, salads, and soufflés which the chef daily rustled up.

One morning, she shared the library with an elderly man who smoked cigars and drank coffee while he read by the window. She caught him looking at her. He jiggled the cigar. "Bother you?"

"I like the smell."

"No, you don't." He doused the brown stump in his coffee. "I got here yesterday. When did you come?"

"Three weeks ago."

"Perhaps you'll show me the ropes."

"Pardon?"

"Tell me where things are, explain to me how things work." He was bald, plump, and his nice, wicked smile was composed of small, overlapping, tobacco-stained teeth.

She recognized English dentistry. His accent was less sure: some sounds seemed English, others American. "I'll show you what I know. It's not much." She went over and extended her hand. "Melanie Minolitte."

He started to get up but shook his head to show he had the disposition but not the energy for courtesy. "I'm Wendell Spear. And you're named after Olivia de Havilland?"

"So Mother said. Though I think I'm more like Scarlett."

Well, not Vivien Leigh, thought Spear. This girl was handsome, not beautiful, a big girl—the word Spear's mind used for all women under fifty, though Amelia had long ago stopped him from saying it, at least around her. Melanie was shaped a bit like the hill across the lake: sloping shoulders, strong torso under a green Italian sack, from which stretched her impressive, boatlike Reeboks. Her tight gold braids resembled those in the Leonardo portrait of Ginevra da Benci, but she was two kilos and much exercise from that demure beauty.

"Where did you see the movie?"

"Rosario, in Argentina. Don't tell me you've heard of it."

"It does sound familiar, but I'm no traveler."

"You're here."

"Not traveling. Settling. Thinking of settling."

"And where were you settled?"

"The Malibu hills, near Los Angeles."

"Really? We go there next fall. Hansl, my companion, will be visiting professor of law."

"Splendid. I'd be there as well, but I just lost my house. In a fire."

"How awful for you. I'm so sorry."

Thought Spear, Is there anything in the universe better than a sweet girl? "Maybe I'll buy another one. On Lake Como. Want to help me look?"

"Yes, absolutely. I'm a good looker."

"That you are."

"You must be very learned to be here. Or are you a Spouse?"

"Neither learned nor Spouse. I'm the visiting antique."

"Is it the fire that's depressed you, or are you just modest?"

"It's the English habit. Success is hated there, bragging went out with *Beowulf*," and to her puzzlement, "Our noisy Anglo-Saxon epic. Modesty's supposed to put people at ease. Of course, it usually annoys or bores them."

"I'm sure you don't do either. You must have a specialty to be here. Philosophy?"

"I was a minor film critic. Oops. I'll stop my little act. I wrote a couple of books."

"That's important."

"Not as important as house hunting."

[2]

After supper—lake trout, tortellini, salad, Pinot Grigio, fruit, and cheese, served to the thirty-five Fellows by four waiters—Spear took himself off to a sheeted plank more like a punishment than a bed. (He'd written in advance that he needed a hard mattress.) After a few reflections on Melanie's large body not all that many yards away down the hall though but inches away—if away at all—from the even larger and blonder body of the German legal scholar Hansl Pflister, Spear sank into the melancholy conviction that the fire had punished him for not following the best part of his nature. He'd settled too early for security and pleasure. The worst of it was that this wasted life was more comedy than tragedy, for, he told himself, It isn't as if Shakespeare had become a butcher and glove maker like his father instead of a playwright.

Step by small step, Spear had made his life smaller and smaller. He'd always felt himself small, and that's the way the fire had treated him. Now he was glad that he was too old to change. Age exonerated him from trying. The eighteenth-century folio saved from the fire was a translation of Aristotle, and Spear had read there remarkable words about old men: *They love as though they will one day hate, and hate as though they will one day love. . . . They think but never know.* "Some of us just want to avoid trouble," he explained to Aristotle. "But an old man doesn't have to be Old Man just as someone who's failed doesn't have to be a Failure." The thought of Melanie's body wasn't an old man's thought. What would happen if one night, Hansl off to some conference, he, Spear, knocked on Melanie's door?

On that, he went to sleep, though he knew that there'd be no knock, either on her door or his.

[3]

The rain was spectacular, thrashing the lake, scalloping the waves, touching off waterfalls in the mountains. Then, boom, it was over, sunlight demisting everything; everything forgiven. No wonder history kept coming back to this place.

Spear shook puffs of shaving cream flecked with white bristles over the ironwork balcony. As beautiful a view as he'd ever seen, different every day as wind and clouds played with air and water. On the clearest days, he could see the snowcap of Mount Blanc. The beauty of the place, its splendor and serenity, revived the feelings he'd had coming to Paris and Italy in his twenties, the pride in being not English but European, Nietzsche's Good European, beyond class origins, the child and father of high culture. He delighted in the fellowship of the Fellows (who were American, Asian, and African as well as European women and men). The good meals, gabbing over Italian wines, the postprandial drift to the terrace for brandy and cigars, made a society finer than he'd ever known.

In the third week, however, he began having his head- and stomachaches. He stopped smoking, then drinking, surrendering brandy first, then wine, finally coffee. He was now eating very little and feeling better, but, one day, after swallowing a spoonful of onion soup, he keeled over.

[4]

Keneret flew to Milan, then drove to Como with the ambulance he'd hired to transport Spear to the Milan airport from the Ospedale San Giovanni. He was not going to let his friend be operated on thousands of miles away from California in the hospital of a small Italian city. "I'm bringing him back," he'd told Amelia Abarbanel on the phone.

"I'm so grateful, Uncle Ez," she said. "If you don't mind my not going over, I'll meet you in California. I can't thank you enough."

"I'm doing it for me, sweetie. I'm not ready to lose your father's surly company."

Spear needed neither ambulance to—nor hospital berth on—the plane. He'd been sedated but was alert and, within minutes, dressed and ready to fly home. "You thought you'd be taking back an invalid."

"A vegetable," said Keneret. "A cigar-smoking zucchini."

"I'm afraid it's no more cigars," said Spear. "As for zucchini, we'll see what happens in L.A. At least you will."

Keneret draped Spear's old blazer around his shoulders. "I think we could use a wheelchair to get you to the car."

"Your arm will do."

Spear shuddered when he saw the ambulance, but it turned out to be useful: he lay on the gurney and slept the half-hour ride to Linati.

[5]

In the first days after the operation, Spear couldn't speak. His head flesh was swollen and livid, the small eyes, which had darted emptily this way and that, now fixed on visitors' faces. No words came out, but he did make almost-intelligible noises, even scribbled on a pad, sometimes a word or two that could be read, but mostly curlicues and wavy lines, small and neat like his handwriting, but scribbles, not letters.

Keneret drew up a chart of words and short sentences at which he thought Spear could at least point. Next to *I want*, he wrote "water," "Kleenex," "newspaper," "magazines," "Jennifer," "Amelia," "a nurse," "a doctor," "painkiller," and so on. Next to *I am*, the list read "hot," "cold," "thirsty," "hungry," "uncomfortable," "all right," "in bad shape," and so on. He held the chart up to Spear's swollen face and pointed to the words that would complete the sentences to see if Spear could blink or otherwise acknowledge his wants.

"I don't think he's seein' real good," said Clary, one of the day nurses, a large black woman who talked to Spear as if he were a four-year-old: "Now Wendell, don't you fuss with that tube. You want Clary to tie your hands?"

Jennifer seemed to get the clearest reaction—smiles—from her grandfather, but she said, "I'm not sure he follows what we say."

By the end of the third week, the catheters, Foleys, and NGs were out of Spear's nose, arms, and penis, and, assisted, he was able to walk up and down the hall. His head size had diminished, and he talked well enough to be understood, though he couldn't talk for long. "I don't remember anything shince the operation, don't remember you coming to shee me. I found the chart you made. Sho good of you. I'm going to keep it."

Keneret liked that. It meant Spear was looking ahead. Days before, he'd emitted the stale odor of death; and everything in and about him seemed to say, *It's finished.* A great hunk of his throat and the musculature in his right arm had been cut out; radiation had lumped, swollen, and twisted him. Now he joked, mostly about his own decay. *Vulture to his own carrion* was the ugly phrase that came to Keneret. He watched his friend rub away at his sore arm, jabbing a forefinger to dislodge black plaques of unsalivated flesh in his wounded mouth. "Not a pretty spectacle," he reported to Marcia, who was so disturbed by her two visits that she gave up coming to the hospital.

[6]

In the fifth postoperative week, Spear was discharged and settled by Jennifer and Amelia next door to the Kenerets in the freshly scrubbed and painted Iwinaga house. (Mr. Iwinaga had died, and Mrs. Iwinaga had been carried off by her daughter to Woodland Hills, where, she told Marcia—who'd been devastated by the departure of this oldest and best of neighbors—"Nothing glow. Like desert.") Spear, weak as he was, relished Mrs. Iwinaga's sacred shrub and had Lourdes—who helped out his two regular nurses—tell her that he would have it attended to properly. Indeed, George, a bulky forty-year-old nurse whom Amelia had plucked from the hospital pool, watered the organic and tidied the inorganic elements of the bush, but, by the time his stint with Spear concluded, it had lost most of its bizarre distinction.

George was soon the indispensable person in Spear's entourage. He entertained Spear's visitors and kept him and them as cheerful as possible. He served the coffee Lourdes brewed from Kenya beans, a fifty-pound sack of which Leet de Loor had bought for him at Trader Joe's. While Lourdes guarded Spear, George drove around to fetch the exotic goodies with which, at the beginning, he tried to rouse his patient's appetite. "His appetite for life," he told the Kenerets and Abarbanels. Spear could barely sip the black brew, but, nose unimpaired, he sniffed its puissant fumes.

"Almosht as good as shigars," he told Leet in his thick, difficult postsurgical speech. (It was not just altered phonemes which came from his mouth: his forefinger constantly excavated the black bits of plaque.)

"Cigars," said Amelia. "They started the cancer."

"Maybe it wush alwaysh there, waiting to come out." Spear pointed toward his cup. "More fumesh pleash, George."

George was a specialist in "the terminal." "Though aren't we all that?" he said cheerfully. Few of his clients lived in houses decorated with mementos of studios and stars, honorary degree certificates, and framed dust jackets. The Kenerets told him that these were only what Spear had stored away and thus saved from the fire. "It's living history," George said. "I adore it."

He reported Spear's doings, which were largely gustatory. "Wendell had eggs for lunch."

"How were they, Wendell?" asked Keneret.

"Like me, shcrambled."

"Ha, ha, ha. What a joker he is." George laughed from the adjacent room, where, in his rare free time when there were visitors, he read a biography of Marlene Dietrich. "I guess you and I are the only people she never fucked," he said to Spear. "Or should I speak only for myself?"

It was hard to imagine George in any woman's bed, though, long ago, Spear learned not to be surprised by any sexual alliance or proclivity. "I mished my chanshe." A cough, a jab at his mouth, which George irrigated with antibiotic wash. "If she could only shee me now."

"You'd knock her for a loop."

No one but Jennifer, Amelia, Leet, and the Kenerets was closer to Spear than George and his evening replacement, Lucia. Like George, she was a recruit from the nurses' pool. Gentle, indefatigable, she had come north from Guatemala twenty years ago. Like George, she loved caring for terminal patients, even when, as in Spear's case, she grew so fond of them that she had to take days off after they died.

George, Lucia, and occasionally Lourdes answered the phones, helped Spear with his correspondence and bills, prepared the cans of Senilac, his chief nourishment, bathed him, toileted him, and, when his speech disintegrated even more, interpreted it for others. Keneret felt that despite its tragic basis, it was a happy household.

[7]

Amelia, who'd returned to St. Louis, was in the air, flying back to Santa Monica, when Spear died. As it happened, Jennifer too was away, the first weekend she hadn't had to work. When, a week earlier, she'd leaned over her shrunken grandfather to tell him that she and Jay were driving down to Palm Springs for the weekend, she'd managed to make out the last words of his she would hear: "Have a good trip, darling." She kept herself from saying, "You too, Grandpa."

At the visit before that, Spear, in bed, followed her with his small, black, watery eyes but said nothing, till Lucia encouraged him to speak. He muttered something. Jennifer leaned close but couldn't make it out; Lucia, however, could.

"I know what he's saying, Miss Jennifer. It's from a book he likes. He pointed it out for me, and I marked it."

Spear nodded yes. It was Shakespeare, and Jennifer too now recognized one of her grandfather's favorites. She read it aloud. It was from *All's Well That Ends Well*, lines that the wicked boaster Captain Parolles speaks after his plot has been exposed and he's been stripped of his captaincy. He begs for his life and, after it's granted, says:

> *If my heart were great,*
> *'t would burst at this. Captain I'll be no more,*
> *but I will eat and drink and sleep as soft*
> *as captain shall. Simply the thing I am*
> *shall make me live.*

[8]

That night, at home, Jennifer read and reread the lines till she felt that she understood why her grandfather's self-deprecation and love of life had fused in this expression of reform and self-acceptance.

[9]

Two weeks later, at his funeral service, she read the lines aloud.

★ ★ ★ ★

SUBJECT: Ezra Keneret; film director; nominated three times for Academy Award. Palme d'Or, Cannes 1960 (*Lianne Takes Jimmy*)

BORN: August 24, 1930, New York, N.Y.

MARRIED:

1. Elizabeth, March 1952; div. Feb. 6, 1969
2. Marcia, March 12, 1969

DIED: April 17, 2004. Santa Monica, Calif.

THE KENERET STORY: A gifted man who, after thirty-five productive years, lost his occupation and his way. His successes were undercut by self-doubt, his failures by successes. A success of failure, a failure of success.

AUTHOR: André Sfaxe, b. 1961, Los Altos, Calif., B.A. UCal, Santa Cruz

FILM WRITER, DIRECTOR: *Twisting*, 2002; *Who Better*, 2004; *Nags*, 2006

FILM CRITICISM: *Sight and Sound; Film Review; Slate*

QUOTE: Like Keneret, I remember any film better than all but a few books. I recognize film voices from movies I saw when I was four. I can put names to a thousand actors, two hundred directors. I worked with and respected Ezra Keneret more than any director of his era. My book uses him and his work to examine the films of that era and my own.

From A. R. Sfaxe, *Keneret: Resumé and Residue*
(University of California Press–Berkeley, 2007)

LEET ★ Ups and Downs

[1]

Leet no longer flipped through microfilm and court records in antiquated archives but sat in a comfortable digitalized office off San Vincente, drumming up trade and supervising a growing group of historians and network virtuosi. She had ideas about starting a school for company historians, sending them cross-country and overseas. In monthly staff meetings, she and the historians worked out techniques for writing the quasi-anthropological histories of companies, communities, neighborhoods, families. They did biographies, not of celebrities or even heads of companies, but of ordinary people, grandmothers and fathers whose affectionate or dutiful offspring could afford a twenty-thousand-dollar commemoration. History, Inc.—the successor of HAL, Inc.—"won't drive," said Agnes, its vice-president, "genealogists out of business. We're not riding in their ruts. These are real family histories, real biographies." She and Leet taught the tricks of research to their mostly amateur historians, young and old. The company was written up in the L.A. *Times* and featured on NPR and public television. Some of Leet's own story, France to Fiji, Keneret, Spear and Dillon to HAL, Inc., was part of the L.A. scene.

Their office had become an electronic library, indexed, cross-referenced, in—what was still called—*touch* with the trillion deposits of potentially significant data. They developed their own systems, worked out their own software, were on-line with the Mormon genealogical records; municipal, marine, insurance, and church archives; newspaper morgues; college magazines; society columns; and family records. They were a web before the Web.

Five years after serving her last pastrami sandwich at the deli, Leet headed a company that included seventy-five historians, was worth twenty-four million dollars, and would soon be worth much more.

[2]

The idea for the early videographies was Hypatia's. At first, Leet said they couldn't do it: buying equipment and materials, hiring cameramen, and creating a small studio were beyond their means, but Hypatia learned—from Oscar and Sylvan Harmel—how to find cut-rate equipment and supplies and expert if, sometimes, superannuated craftsmen. Young technicians they'd find themselves. Agnes said, "Let's go for it."

Said Leet, "We'll try one out."

The one was a bar mitzvah gift, *The Early Life and Times of Steven Rosenblatt*. The Rosenblatts had a larger-than-usual family archive of movies, videos, and photographs going back almost a century. Hypatia intercut the best of them with the filmed ceremony. Sylvan and Agnes wrote commentary which was interspersed with family interviews. There were Technicolor and black-and-white sequences of Mother Rosenblatt riding a horse, driving off with baby Steven to the market, and presiding over—a slightly rehearsed—family dinner. Daddy Rosenblatt was filmed in his advertising agency, at the phone and computer, golfing, surfing, and playing tennis with Steven and sister Selma. Hypatia edited the footage as if it were *Citizen Kane*. The seventy-five-minute result, shown at a large party, generated twenty orders.

"It's a real feature," said an amazed, delighted Oscar. (Sylvan had to persuade him not to screen it for their father.)

A year later, HAL, Inc., overflowed with personal and institutional video commissions. They no longer rented but owned equipment and had a small house staff of craftsmen and technicians. A floor of their Westwood office building was taken up by videography; two years later, their video profit alone was twenty-two million dollars.

[3]

It was at the reception after Spear's funeral that Leet ran into the young Argentine woman whose skein of improbable threads resembled her own: Argentina, New York, Munich, Italy, and Los Angeles, where Hansl, her companion, was visiting professor of comparative law at the UCLA Law School. They'd read Spear's obituary in the *L.A. Times* and come to the funeral.

Dark-eyed, robust Melanie Minolitte had, it seems, known Spear in his forty days at the Lake Como Center, had even been at the table with him when he'd keeled over, and had, with Hansl, accompanied him in the ambulance to the hospital in Como where he'd had the biopsy which revealed the cancer.

"The first two weeks, I helped him look for houses," she told the surprised Leet. "He spoke much about the house he'd lost in a fire, but he was usually funny even about that. I laughed all the time with him. I don't think he really wanted a house, it just gave him an excuse to take boats around the lake. But we did look for them, big ones, little ones. We also looked at churches, had lunch, and drank too much. Till he got sick."

"I took dictation from him," Leet told her. "For the book he wrote about Mr. Keneret's films. The first week, I couldn't understand half the words he used. He never got impatient, he enjoyed explaining things more than writing them."

Said Melanie, "In the last two weeks, he talked very little. I think the cancer was already in his mouth. He'd given up those horrible cigars, the only thing about him I didn't like."

Jennifer came up to Melanie, "Your friend just told me that you knew my grandfather in Italy."

"We did, yes. A short but beautiful friendship. I was very moved by your—*elogio.*"

"Eulogy," said Sylvan, who'd joined them. "It was perfect, Jenny. Wendell would have loved it."

"It was his Shakespeare."

Melanie said, "I understand your feeling. My grandfather is, after Hansl, my best friend."

"Is he here in L.A. with you?" asked Jennifer.

"No, he's back in Rosario. That's our city in Argentina."

Leet, gulping, said, "I think I know someone there."

"I'm amazed," said Melanie. "Nobody here or in Europe has heard of it. You have an Argentine friend there?" Looking at Leet, who flushed, then paled. "Are you all right?"

"Yes, just surprised."

Sylvan said, "It's your father, isn't it? The film you were making with Ez when you came here."

Leet said that it was. She looked closely at Melanie's sympathetic face. "I'll explain to you."

Melanie took the trembling wineglass from this slender Frenchwoman's hand and held it. "If you want to, please."

[4]

The dining room of the Rosario Jockey Club, wainscoted, medallioned, pillared, and beflagged, was, except for waiters in formal dress and herself at a table full of heavy silverware, empty. The minutes waiting for her father there came close to stopping her heart. Part of it was fatigue and jet lag, though she'd spent the night in Buenos Aires at a hotel on Maipú and flown into Rosario this morning. There were supposedly a million people in this city, but at least from the airport to the Jockey Club, it looked as small as Tarbes. The taxi drove along the banks of the Peronio River, mud brown in harsh air. The windows of the old Plymouth taxicab were open; she smelled but could not see roses.

"Roses? *Flores?*" she asked the driver.

"*Un arbol. Jacaranda.*"

"*Entiendo.*"

There were other flowering trees, something like hyacinths, a field of sunflowers, and another in which enormous red squirrels scooted up gnarled trees. Finally, houses, wooden with trellises, then larger ones with driveways and stone lions.

[5]

It was the man who now called himself Pedro de Lloer who'd chosen the Jockey Club. When Leet told Melanie, she'd said, "Well, it's not as isolated as the middle of the pampas."

Sylvan, next to Leet, as he frequently was now, said, "Sure you don't want a traveling companion?"

"Thank you, Sylvan, but of all the things I've done, this is one I have to do by myself."

Agnes, who with Melanie and, later, Jennifer, had made most of the inquiries and calls which led to de Lloer, had also offered to accompany her. "This may not be like these television reunions. You might need a witness. Even protection."

"If I do, it means I don't understand anything at all. I won't need—I can't have—anything but him and me."

Using an Ariadne gift for the network labyrinth, Agnes had traced the transformation of the French citizen Pieter de Loor into the Argentine businessman Pedro de Lloer. She'd learned about his business—a brewery—his wife and two sons, one of whom had died a few years ago, age eighteen. Jennifer—who was now house counsel for History, Inc.—had checked out Leet's legal position in Argentine, French, U.S., and international law. She'd also helped get her an emergency visa.

Leet made the telephone call and, when Señor de Lloer came to the phone, said in French, "This is a voice from the past."

"No *hablar francés*," said the voice.

"Oh, Papa, this is Leet."

Silence, then the line went dead.

It was Sylvan and Melanie who told her that she must go to Rosario. "You can't do such a thing by phone," Sylvan said. "It's seeing that's believing."

"And touching," said Melanie. "You have to touch each other."

"He won't see me, let alone touch me."

"He will," said Sylvan. "I know about strange fathers. He was shocked when you told him. It was too much. You came back into his life without warning, like a mugger."

"My God, maybe he had a heart attack on the phone. I gave him a heart attack. He's dead."

"You know that's silly," said Sylvan.

"I'll find out," said Melanie. "I'll call my grandfather."

The next day, she called Leet. "My grandfather knows one of the distributors of his beer. If you say so, he'll ask de Lloer to see you."

"That'll shame him," said Leet. "He'll hate me even more."

"He'll see you. He doesn't hate you," said Sylvan.

"I can't force him. I have no right to expect anything. I don't even know if I want anything. I've gotten along without him for over twenty years."

"These reunions end in tears and kisses. They won't be able to pry you apart."

[6]

She did not recognize an atom of the old man with white hair and mustache who walked slowly into the dark-paneled dining room past bowing waiters. This man in his pin-striped black suit was not just older than she'd have guessed her father would be but smaller and thinner. Papa had been an athlete; this man with the white hair and rheumy brown eyes—hadn't Papa's been green?—looked as if he'd never been able to move faster than a worm. She rose to shake his hand or receive an embrace and saw that she was taller than he.

"I was sure it was a mistake," she told Sylvan later. "I thought he might be someone Papa had sent in his place. Then he said, in English, "How do you do, Aleitha?' and held out this liver-spotted old hand, which I took like I was closing a deal."

Sylvan said, "But you felt something, something you recognized."

"Everything made for distance, need, fear, fatigue, uncertainty, let alone twenty-odd years, and then, English! He chose a language to separate us, just as he picked that gloomy club. All around us, the waiters, the empty tables with the monogrammed china and silver."

"But it was your father."

"He said there was something in him that loved me, but that if he opened it up, he'd crack, and so would I. It wasn't as if we could see each other every day or even once a month so that we could become what we once were. We'd each made lives far apart from the other. 'My fault. My choice,' he said. 'Seeing you brings up what I'm too old to bear now.' 'What is that, Papa?' He trembled when I said that. 'Guilt,' he said. I said, 'Isn't there something stronger than guilt? I am yours.'

"'A leaf from my tree. Nature doesn't make paternity or companion-ship or love. Because you have my—my chemistry doesn't mean you should love me, or I you. Love is choice, not nature. If you need to hear the word *love* from me, I'll say it, but to feel it, I'd have to undo myself.'

"'*Je comprends bien*, Papa. Or have I no right to call you that?'

"'If it pleases you, eases you, I have no right to refuse it.' We were talk-ing French now, 'But I can't act as your father anymore. Even the once-a-month father I was in Meillac. You have a right, a legal right, to part of what I leave. I'll see that you get it. I should have done it before. I won't explain my life here now. Much of it has been undoing, forgetting, try-ing to forget the life I had, the person I was. Four years ago, I lost a son here, Jacobo, to the same politics that lost me you, Marc, your mama, myself. I had nothing to do with politics here, but I'm the father of a boy who was, as they mendaciously, horribly, say here, *disappeared*. When I learned that he'd never come back, that this boy would have no more life, something in me understood that I'd never stop paying for having— however indirectly—disappeared other fathers' sons.

"'A life ago, two lives ago, I was a—what?—literary boy, a reader, me the son of a *flamand* peasant. Reading made me a truer Frenchman than many who made fun of and hated me. What do you know, what should you know, of the deadness and rot I thought—sixty years ago—was France? My head, like lots of literary—and nonliterary—heads, was on fire with the politics in Italy and Germany. For such a literary boy to read Céline—do you even know his name?—even such brilliant filth as *Bagatelles pour un massacre*, praised by André Gide—you know that name from school'—I did, we'd read something—'and other so-called im-mortals, well, I was on fire. I too believed that the—the Yids were run-ning and ruining France. I won't go on with this history—this excuse— there are books you can read, but there it was. After I passed the *bac*,

I worked for our deputy, and then—I was so proud—I did what I did. I made my own noose. So my life'—he threw up his hands, wildly; I felt this white-haired old man uncorking what he'd bottled up, doing it for me—'became filth, and when I tried to make another one, I could only make it out of the old filth. The opposite of what I wanted to do. I couldn't lose myself. Then the virus, the same virus, came here, to this country, and what happened? I lost the best of what I had. Everything new, everything good, disappeared into the filth I'd spent twenty years trying to escape. I tried to disappear and they disappeared my, my—' and he couldn't get out the word *son*.

"I wanted to reach across the table and touch his face, but there was such cold coming from it. I said, 'You weren't ever that way with me. You were kind, *doux*, generous, loving, a wonderful papa. It was such a good, sweet time when you came.'

"'I was happy once to have a daughter and son to kiss and hold a few times a year in that angry village. And I loved your mother—though I can hardly say the word *love* now. If I ever think back—I try not to, but it happens—I tell myself that I left you out of love, knowing that when the village knew about me, they would turn on you.'

"'Why didn't we move to Tarbes, Papa? Or Paris? Or anywhere? New York?' He didn't say anything. 'Why, Papa?'

"'Why? I lived like a rodent in the dark, and that's what I became. I had no money, no energy, no will. At twenty-three, I'd been a superman, part of the New Order; at forty-three, I was a coward, a sneak. When that book came out, and *Le Monde* uncovered a new villain, *un mouchard*, *un pleurnicheur*, it was all over. I did—so I told myself—the one brave thing of my life. I left the sweetness of my life, your mama, my son, my little daughter. But I did it without thinking how they would feel. How you'—looking at me for the first time really—'would feel. I thought only of what—I believed—would happen to the family of the Flemish traitor. It was done like lightning. Callous? Yes. I was already callous. And I've thickened that callus for twenty-five years. Only when Jacobo was disappeared—for a while. . . . But my heart was so thick with it, I recovered. If it can be said that there is an I to recover.'

"I said, 'Papa, I think I understand—.' He interrupted me, 'Why should you understand or believe anything I say? The only truth in my life now comes in dreams. These I can't disappear. In them, sometimes, I see you, *ma chere petite fille,* but when I wake up, if I remember that, I—I try—try not to.' He got up. 'I can't stay.' He held out his hand. 'Papa,' I said. 'May I kiss you good-bye?' His face was cold, the lips under the white mustache like ice, but he opened his arms. I went into them, held him. It was like holding a snowman. I recognized nothing, no scent, no warmth. The arms folded around me, and there was a sound I want to think was a sob, then he walked out of the room. I watched the bent back of an old man in a pin-striped suit."

★　★　★　★

CALIFORNIA　To throw an animal by tripping it.

From *The Dictionary of American Regional English*,
Frederick Cassidy, chief editor (Belknap Press, 1985)

CODA ★ Quake

Sylvan had just returned from Ezra Keneret's funeral. Leet, pregnant again, had felt too ill to go but had written a note to Marcia which Sylvan delivered. It was after midnight, she was asleep, although she'd gotten up at eleven because the baby cried and wouldn't stop crying. Since she wasn't wet or thirsty, Leet thought it must have been a bad dream, but later, after the quake, she told Sylvan that she thought that Jessie, like a bird or field animal, had felt something. "A little seismograph."

She and Sylvan were shaken out of bed. Floor, walls, the whole house shook and shook; and more than the house. Sylvan, who'd grown up in California, knew in three seconds what it was, though, like Leet, was terrified. Her almost-instantaneous second reaction was for the baby. She leapt from the shaking floor and ran half drunkenly across the hall. The house was already filled with crashes.

"Shoes," yelled Sylvan. "You'll be cut."

The dresser had fallen over, toys were all over the floor, the room shook madly as she dove under the wildly swinging mobile to get the baby. "Jessie, Jessie." In the small glow of the night-light, Jessie's blue eyes were huge. Even as Leet thought, Thank God, she's all right, and picked her up, the lights went out.

Sylvan half led, half carried them into the bathroom where they stood on the lintel holding one another while the rollicking percussion smashed, broke, and, slowly, a piece here, a piece there, collapsed the house. The baby's heart pounded so that Leet found herself pushing it back into the soft chest.

Though the quake lasted but forty-five seconds, the thickness, intensity, and strangeness of events transformed their time sense. The rumble seemed forever.

Then, blessed miracle, it was, briefly, over. Sylvan knelt to put Leet's sandals on her trembling feet, then made his way through fallen, fractured displaced beams, glass, and a chaos of breakage to the pantry for the earthquake kits—flashlights, bottled water, Band-Aids, antibiotics. (He'd forgotten there was a kit feet away in the bathroom.) His sandals crunched the glass of windows, pictures, dishes, television, and computer monitors.

Clutching each other, Leet and the baby stayed still, trembling. Jessie sobbed like a grown person. Sylvan brought them bottled water. "Yes, I'm—." Leet couldn't remember the word *parched*. She gave Jessie water, then drank herself. Sylvan was back in the wreckage, flashlight picking out teddy bears, diapers, lamps, wires. In the broken kitchen, the refrigerator lay on its back, like a dead polar bear. He pulled it open and found a plastic bottle of formula. "She'll have to take it cold," he told Leet. "I better check everything."

"Stay."

"I'll be careful."

The baby sucked milk. Leet, holding her, sank to the floor. Her hand moved over her daughter's small back, head, cheek, forehead, chest. "It's all right, darling. Everything's all right. Daddy's fixing everything." Her stomach was spinning. What was this doing to—what would turn out to be—her second daughter?

In what had been their dining room, Sylvan saw an orange glow, which he first thought was a reflection. It was flame. Mind in exile, he forgot there were fire extinguishers everywhere. Instead, he found a soup bowl, filled it at the intact kitchen sink. "Thank God, there's water." He poured it on the flame and went back for more. Four times, he made the trip and, in this strange way, extinguished the fire. Using the flashlight, he found what started it, a jar of kitchen matches which had been ignited by a square of wall hurled at them by the grinding plates miles below their hill.

"The bizarre thing," he said later, "was that, after a minute, nothing in particular seemed bizarre. I only thought, I have to get us out of here." With the mechanics of instinct, he maneuvered Leet and Jessie through the lightless rubble.

Outside, the three-plus Harmels sat on the grass near a grove of swinging palms. Till they lit flashlights, they were in layers of dark. Power was out everywhere. The lights lit bits of their tilted, crunched house.

Then the rumbling started again, the three of them screamed while, under them, the hill shook. "We have to go," said Leet. "Go."

"How? Where? The roads could be gone."

They hadn't even noticed if their cars were there, let alone intact.

Holding each other and the suddenly sleeping baby, Leet and Sylvan felt each other shivering, trembling, breathing.

"It's safer here," he managed, then 'here' once again rolled and rollicked, flooding them with terror. They opened their mouths to scream, but deeper even than terror was their parental being, so that they only moaned and held on to Jessie as if she were not only what needed but was their support.

In the world that had lost structure, they were each other's structure. They leaned against each other, parched, tense, exhausted, in a half trance of terror, but, in the deepest way ever, together.

ACKNOWLEDGMENTS

In one form or another, sections of this book and sections related to it have appeared in the following publications: *Agni, Antioch Review, Iowa Review, Marlboro Review, On the Make, Paris Review, Southwest Review, TriQuarterly,* and *Yale Review.*

ABOUT THE AUTHOR

Richard Stern was born in 1928 in New York City and published his first novel, *Golk,* in 1960. Among his many works are the novels *Europe, or Up and Down with Schreiber and Baggish* and *Other Men's Daughters*; the short-story collections *Packages* and *Noble Rot: Stories 1949–1988*; and the memoir *A Sistermony.* In 1985 he won the Medal of Merit for the Novel given by the American Academy and Institute of Arts and Letters. Stern is a frequent contributor to *Partisan Review* and the *New York Times* and has taught English for many years at the University of Chicago.